A
LIST

Also by Helen Weinzweig

Basic Black with Pearls
A View from the Roof

PASSING
CEREMONY

HELEN WEINZWEIG

LIST

First published in Canada in 1973 by House of Anansi Press
Published in Canada in 2017 and the USA in 2017 by House of Anansi Press Inc.
www.houseofanansi.com

House of Anansi Press is committed to protecting our natural environment.
As part of our efforts, the interior of this book is printed on paper that contains
100% post-consumer recycled fibres, is acid-free, and is processed chlorine-free.

21 20 19 18 17   1 2 3 4 5

Library and Archives Canada Cataloguing in Publication

Weinzweig, Helen, 1915–, author
Passing ceremony / Helen Weinzweig.
Issued in print and electronic formats.
ISBN 978-1-4870-0260-2 (softcover). — ISBN 978-1-4870-0261-9 (EPUB).—
ISBN 978-1-4870-0262-6 (EPUB)

I. Title.

PS8595.E45P3 2017   C813'.54   C2017-901310-6
                        C2017-901311-4

Library of Congress Control Number: 2017933805

Series design: Brian Morgan
Cover illustration: Jessica Fortner

*We acknowledge for their financial support of our publishing program
the Canada Council for the Arts, the Ontario Arts Council, and the Government of
Canada through the Canada Book Fund.*

Printed and bound in Canada

PASSING CEREMONY

INTRODUCTION AND MEMOIR
by James Polk

IN THE SUMMER OF 1971, I received a large Birks box meant for custom jewellery, neatly tied in ribbon, directed to "Editor" at House of Anansi Press, then situated on a down-market Toronto backstreet between gay baths and a motorcycle gang clubhouse. Intrigued by such luxury packaging, I found inside a stack of quality bond paper, perfectly typed, with a note advising me to throw the pages into the air and arrange them as they fell. Chance, "aleatoric" fiction? Maybe in New York or Paris, but would the Coles bookstores or staid Britnell's stock anything unbound? I skimmed the fragments, without throwing pages around and without much interest. Soon I couldn't put them down.

The action seemed to centre upon a weird Rosedale wedding, with a gay but closeted groom, a promiscuous bride, and a Greek chorus of unhappy upper-class voices brooding about age, betrayals, and shattered illusions. The dialogue crackled. "Now I know you're a psychiatrist. You have no imagination." "Pure loves don't need church weddings. They could have spiritual intercourse anywhere."

I noted the suicides, bad sex, and abortions haunting the privileged guests, the mad grandmother imprisoned upstairs, and the cadre of enraged women. The bride's fatuous father returns with a Mexican wife, eighteen years old, who nurses her baby sitting on the floor among the guests, hiding her head under a rebozo. The father explains to his daughter that "in Mexico the women mature early. They bloom briefly, oh so briefly, my dear." The bride snaps back: "She is not much older than when I bloomed briefly. You sent me away. You had my baby taken from me." I turned more loose pages. "If you know my mother," says a forlorn business man to his coy mistress, "you will understand me."

I had to acquire it. I got permission from our usually captious Reading Committee — Anansi was a co-op in those days, sort of — and wrote the author an enthusiastic note. But suddenly I was nervous to meet him or her. Who could have written this stylish, surreal, sometimes savage, often funny cantata of many voices out of Rosedale? Our usual authors wore beads and called me "man." Our backlist featured manuals for dodging the U.S. draft, for beating a drug rap or fighting the Spadina expressway. I rearranged the slush pile of manuscripts and dusty pizza boxes into a quasi-office, and before long, in came Helen Weinzweig, sparkling, fresh, over fifty, sporting a Holt Renfrew suit and a gleaming perm, delighted to be an alien among the hippies. She had no trouble with us binding the pages, setting a title, and maybe rearranging the fragments for a clearer story arc. "Oh, sorry, I have to write in flashes, and get it down quickly." She paused for a throaty, self-mocking laugh — "If I don't, it will all go with me."

I signed her up immediately.

Passing Ceremony was the first novel I edited, and how lucky was that? Helen was smart, wise, and funny, and flexible within reason. Her literary models were an education for me. Dead serious about literary style, she had read everybody from Conrad to Beckett to Ionesco and beyond. She was a fan of the French *nouveau roman*, the latest anti-fictions of Robbe-Grillet, Duras, Sarraute, and other French savants who eschewed the dated, bourgeois novels of description and plot, preferring fragments, suggestions, snapshots. Also influential was surrealist Luis Buñuel, and the new wave of European films from Antonioni, Godard, and Fellini; thus *Passing Ceremony* often reads like a movie, with the Rosedalites as stunned and trapped as if lost in Marienbad or Hiroshima. She gave me books by Butor and Ponge so I could understand her more arcane purposes, as well as Rosten's *The Joys of Yiddish*, so I could understand her spiel.

Helen rewrote slowly, meticulous in every word, scrutinizing the position of articles and gerunds, the tone, the exact shades of irony. We went often to the family cottage in Kearney, bringing European angst to the pines and docks, with her husband, John, equally obsessed with his own brilliant art of bi-tonal keys and multiple rhythms. It had not occurred to me that Helen was married to the famous composer, one who had transformed Canadian music from the hymns and larks ascending of what Helen called "British organists" into the sounds of international modernity spurred by Schoenberg, Gershwin, Bartók, and hot jazz. There is a sense that *Passing Ceremony* is a kind of complex chorale of its own, with voices of diverse tones and timbres interweaving.

As a couple, the Weinzweigs were an astounding cultural force, although their long marriage sometimes had a Homeric quality, with many a skirmish and epic jealousies, rages, and comings and goings. They both helped form nationalist organizations—the Canadian Music Centre, the

Writers' Union—and their house on Manor Road became
a mecca for Toronto's creative class, a landmark in the city's
transition from butter tarts and Orange Parades to the bustling, creative, sizzling, maddeningly overpriced metropolis
it has now become.

So who was this avant-garde Eurocentric novelist masquer-
ading as a Jewish housewife in the stolid, solid Toronto of
the '70s? She was originally Polish, like John—born Helen
Tannenbaum in Warsaw, in 1915, to a feisty hairdresser
mother and a fierce Talmudic scholar and Marxist revolutionary father. The marriage was brief, a passing ceremony,
dysfunctional and stormy. The father soon fled the family
for Italy; the mother blackmailed the wealthy, philandering
husband of a beauty-parlour client to stake her passage to
Toronto (1924) with her precocious nine-year-old daughter.
Never shy, she bulled her way into the beauty-parlour business and opened a salon on College Street, between Bathurst
and Spadina—then the Jewish quarter, a hotbed of creative
immigrant energies, sporting delis, rabbis, gangsters, furri-
ers, politicos, and bagels to die for. Their apartment opened
onto a back window at the King Cinema, where Helen got
much of her English (and a gift for dramatic dialogue) from
Hollywood soundtracks. She had come to Canada speaking
only Yiddish, but soon she mastered the British classics, aced
high school, and read everything in sight.

Around 1930, at about fifteen years old, she marched out
on her mother, leaving home to search for her long-lost father,
travelling alone through war-scarred Europe to get to Italy.
She found her Marxist revolutionary scholar, only to be locked
into a back room and held hostage as Father tried to whee-
dle money out of Mother. Eventually the prisoner escaped

through the window and returned home in one piece, but the train trips, the surreal landscapes, the monster father, the uncertainty and fear of this journey haunt much of her later fiction. I suspect that many of the huge cast of *Passing Ceremony* owe their unease to the European past, to generic memories of wartime deprivation and loss.

Back home, there was Mother, and even worse, tuberculosis. Still reverberating from her Italian nightmare, she had to leave for a rural Ontario sanatorium, enduring an exile from civilization for two years and re-emerging with one collapsed lung and a lifelong breathing problem. There had been, however, a benefit— "I read myself silly." She also read herself into a job, memorizing most of Gray's *Anatomy* to qualify for work at a medical office, having no other scientific credentials whatsoever—once again saved by the book. Then one day, on the College streetcar, she ran into an old high school friend, renewed their acquaintance, and, reader, she married him.

John Weinzweig was by then teaching and composing, but also busy cutting pelts in his father's fur shop, located over a store at College and Clinton. With marriage there came at last a semblance of stability: the couple soon enough had two sons, a modest house, and a reasonable income, but Helen predictably grew restless in homemaker land. A therapist advised her to try writing as a way to bring shape to her life, and at this, being Helen, she immediately excelled. Her very first short story was published by *Canadian Forum* in 1967. She was good, but a beginner, at age fifty-two.

"One of the drawbacks of starting when you're older is you know what good writing is, and you know you can't do it," she told the *Globe* in 1990. But she could do it. Everything she submitted to the magazines got published, in those mythic days when short stories had markets and commercial currency, though her age and gender bothered the critics. How could a nice Jewish housewife and mother seriously try writing, a man's game, especially when she was so clearly over the hill? Helen retorted that she was translating male forms fiction "into the female," and letting readers know what "I as a woman feel like." Hard to believe this was ever necessary to spell out, with Canada's long roster of superb women writers, but the revolution crawled on very slowly here.

Passing Ceremony shows us plenty of women angry, abandoned, humiliated, and even brutalized: the bride is routinely insulted by the partygoers for her sins; one lady sneers that she'll soon be back "in business" even when married; an old flame sees her as a "whore in a white dress" and spits in her face in front of everyone. The groom quickly says it was an accident. No one complains; all are polite. It's exhilarating when, after the ceremony, the bride dumps her dreadful social set, throws off her scarlet letter, and opts for a new, real life as an independent being, no longer a cheated daughter or scandalous whore, but a woman reclaimed:

— And I'll have my babies back, poor wee bastards, pushing their way out of bloody wombs, filling their lungs, not knowing their fate.
— We'll make it up to them for having been born.

The last speaker is the groom, mourning Leon, his faithless lover. He weeps for his sister's suicide; he must hide his gayness; he is no queer caricature, but sympathetic and humane, unlike the other male swine at the party. For the homosexual and the despised tramp, it's been hell, but liberation is possible amid the rubble now, and they seize it avidly.

Feminist redemption is the theme of Weinzweig's second (and alas, her last) novel, *Basic Black with Pearls*, which won the City of Toronto Book Award in 1981. The scattered, lonely, gormless heroine wanders Toronto searching for her married lover who (she believes) leaves coded clues for their trysts in the *National Geographic*. By the end, she has ditched her awful husband, given her pearl necklace to his grim mistress, left her redecorated Forest Hill house, and found young, single naturalist Andy, although she knows "there will be risks." What's not to like? I am told that both of Helen's books are staples of women's studies courses now, and I'd like to know how today's female (and male) readers compute the experience of Helen's women as they survive the surreal passing ceremonies offered by the patriarchy and move on out and get a life.

In reading *Passing Ceremony* again, after all these years, I enjoyed the satire and absurdity, and the sure-footed writing that got my attention early on—but I am now also moved by the author's sympathy for her lost tribe, well-off materially but stalked by uncertainty, failure, sexual anxiety, aging, loneliness, illness. They may be nasty to one another, but they are mortally scared.

Not the bride and groom. At the end, the newlyweds leave on their fake honeymoon. They are forced to eat fast food in a chilly car. They end up in a freezing attic, huddled in blankets like war refugees, but they hold hands, are tender with each other. They won't live happily ever after in any ordinary sense, but they are free now, and their last words move the novel out of purgatory and into real action in the real world:

— Ready?
— Ready.

After *Basic Black with Pearls* and a collection of short stories, *The View from the Roof,* Helen was tragically felled by either Alzheimer's disease or a series of small strokes, or both. She slowly lost her intellectual acumen, her memory, her words, and spent the rest of a long life in a home, outliving her husband, cared for by her sons, and passing on at age ninety-four, in 2010. The early loss of her real self, and of her potential for more fine work, is unbearable to contemplate. Yet there is a quasi-rabbinical exchange in *Passing Ceremony* (in fact, you'll find a lot of quasi-rabbinical wisdom strewn throughout the book), which a guest offers to justify the charade of the wedding:

— Love is not enough.
— Nothing is enough.
— You can't have everything.
— Then they did the right thing.
— What?
— Something.

No, we can't have everything, but some of us do something, can have *something*. When the books were first published, critics were favourable, if puzzled and surprised, but I know that many readers found Helen's style quirky and challenging and difficult to understand. Luckily, I think we've caught up to her now. Her total output was indeed small, but what there was is choice, and the reissue of her two wonderful novels by Anansi is a strong sign that the writing has endured. And that her original voice and distinctive eye will not be lost. "When I go," she joked with me that first day, "it will all go with me."

No way.

JAMES POLK was the long-time editorial director at House of Anansi Press, where he worked with Margaret Atwood, Dennis Lee, George Grant, Northrop Frye, Erín Moure, Charles Taylor, Roch Carrier, and many others. After his Harvard Ph.D. he taught English in both the U.S. and Canada, and for twenty years directed government funding in Ontario for books, magazines, theatre, and the arts. He has written literary criticism, reviews, fiction, nonfiction, and a comedy about a small Canadian literary press. He once studied to be a concert pianist and still practises.

To Paul and Daniel

"Now what an odd thing the marriage service is!" said Miles, leaning back and using an almost confidential tone. "I have been reading it. And I can hardly believe that I have heard it pronounced over myself. I mean I had forgotten that part of things. It is only a passing ceremony."

—Ivy Compton-Burnett,
A FATHER AND HIS FATE

...This chapel is damp and makes me shiver. It smells of green mould despite the flowers, despite her perfume. She leans against me like you did when we stood like this many deaths ago. See what you missed Maggie by killing yourself: your brother now takes a woman to be my lawful wedded: a marriage is still possible: you did not wait to find out what is possible: if you could hear me now: with this ring I thee wed and I will not fail you in sickness and in health as all the others did. Abandoned yet haunted by all of you, every night a nightmare of vanished faces, I take her, take thee, a small life, to have and to hold against my impossible longing. The minister says I may kiss your dry lips...

...I take thee all right yes louder I take thee take you for you are willing to be held with this ring having agreed to bind ourselves with golden circles...it is a ritual favored by ancient gods provided we do not look back...I can feel them my confederates in hell hurling their satanic thoughts at my back behind me where latecomers sit who changed their minds at the last minute and the fumes of spite rise to the vaults even the cross no longer deters the devils...I must lean against you and feel your shoulder with mine because separated from you their fire will consume me...why won't they believe I will be faithful to you...

— Such a handsome couple.

— Handsome is as handsome does.

— You never know they may do it handsomely. Differently perhaps yet it can be —

— Of course. But why go through this rigmarole. They shouldn't involve the church.

— Purification. The universal type of love, saintly, none of your sweating kind.

— Pure loves don't need church weddings. They can have spiritual intercourse anytime, anywhere. They could write each other long letters.

— For that matter no one needs a license to love.

— Love is not enough.

— Nothing is enough.

— You can't have everything.

— Then they did the right thing.

— What?

— Something.

Leon's face with the heavy nose keeps getting mixed in with the minister's features. The groom concentrates on the minister's mouth, which is quite unlike Leon's, the one having thin lips while Leon's are full. By watching the mouth, he can follow the marriage ceremony. His head is full of noises, so that the words are not distinct. In the groom's breastpocket is a postcard showing the beach at Malaga. The note on the back reads, Thinking of you and trying to understand. Love, Leon. Not shown on the colored photograph is another part of the beach, where Leon lies on the sand, stroking the olive skin of a slim boy.

The bride is similarly attentive. She knows the litany by heart and can anticipate every word. Still, she is nervous: there is a rustling at the rear of the chapel: latecomers are trying to seat themselves quietly. She senses a certain agitation. Is it her father's presence, has he been recognized? Did he bring his Mexican wife? Behind her back a disquiet like mice at night. Yes, yes, I do, she says when it is her turn to reply.

... All my little ones gone the last of my babies stands there in virginal white making promises she will never keep just like her father... I don't understand what it was all about those long swollen months the black pain now they're gone all of them gone... it isn't fair it isn't fair...

You sit there, father of the bride, you sit there straight and proud. In the middle of a middle row to the right of the aisle. How is it you are not in your rightful place, in the second pew to the left, beside the mother of the bride? It is your son Thomas who sits there in your stead.

You are being examined: more eyes are on you than on your daughter repeating her vows.

Speculations. You are taking an awful risk being here. And if you had to bring your little dark wife, poor child, so young, why did you not dress her properly?

And as sensitive observers we should be registering your deeply moving feelings, or, at the very least, some senti-mental reflections. You are being stubborn. We cannot read you. Give us something to go on: some memories, a few regrets. Alternatively, cogent theories on marriage gleaned from your vast studies: references to tribal customs would be acceptable. Yet nothing of literary interest comes through. No philosophies? We remember you as quite a philosopher, with a tendency to place mundane events in historical, usually ancient Greek, perspective. Surely, this is the very moment...ah...a passing thought: the groom appears to you as a man without bones, the kind whose flesh is as yielding as a woman's; and the idea of those two softnesses copulating is disgusting to you. Too strong? Offensive, merely, then. That will have to do for now. Perhaps, later, at the reception, after a few drinks, we'll get back to you.

Even so, there is a restlessness about the father of the bride.

While his head and shoulders, tilted slightly forward, indicate absolute attention, below, where none can see, he squirms in his seat. His knees are pressed together, his feet to one side, as if sidestepping a puddle. Of course. The father of the bride is experiencing symptoms of enlargements of the prostate gland.

All this time he has been trying to recall whether he had seen anywhere in the underground corridors outside the chapel any sign of a men's toilet. All the solid oak doors with heavy wrought iron ornamentation looked alike. No indication of the nature of their sanctuary. All his concentration is directed towards controlling an urge to void.

Frederick Gainsborough Smith.

Fred.

During the long drive on the 401 Freeway, you were thinking of your birthday, your fiftieth. A half century, half a hundred, fifty, five O. You tried to slough off the obsession with your age, thinking one has no choice over birth or death, or very little else to be honest. Honesty is no help: the figure 50 takes up all the spaces in your head. You can think of nothing else. Still, as you drove at 80 miles an hour, you consoled yourself that you are still alert and well-coordinated, in complete control of the speeding mechanical monster. You were cold, but you left your window rolled all the way down. Your hands were blue on the wheel; your right foot numb on the accelerator. Even as you followed the guiding white line, you were overcome with fear, as on those long night-flights in the war. You felt a compulsion as you did then to keep going, past the target, head out for nowhere and never return. Just the same, you continued on course, today, as always, you did what was expected of you: made all the right decisions, followed the signs, took the correct turns and landed where you were supposed to. So here you are.

The little chapel is cold as a tomb. You look at your watch and realize you made good time: you are a half hour early. You are alone, except for a florist still fiddling with the flowers. The wooden pew resists your efforts to relax. With your coat as a pillow you stretch out on the bench, close your eyes and wish you were home in your own bed. Next week, you lucky man, because it will be your birthday, you will receive pussy for a present. Once a year you get a gratuitous lay. Marylou will hand you a loaded martini and expect you to go to it, boy, you really are quite virile considering your advanced years. Marylou will let you undress her. There will be no resistance. But, unlike you, or perhaps because of you, she will refuse to play passion's fool. Not a word, not a sound, from her, while you, desperate idiot, will make cries like a loon.

How cold it is. You take your coat from under your head and cover yourself with it. You are all alone now. Your head, without support, gets lighter and lighter, you feel dizzy. You sit up. You don't feel well: you might as well go home right after the ceremony, forget the reception, go back to your house, where, if nothing else, there is the safety of indifference. You close your eyes again, you slump as best you can against the straight wooden back, only to have to stand up to allow others to enter your pew.

Later, with all the others, you turn around, you twist your neck, to look back and follow the advance of the bride from the rear of the chapel to the altar. As she is about to pass you, you look up hoping to catch sight of the face that once meant so much to you, but see instead ghostly features behind a veil.

You follow the white figure as she proceeds down the aisle in that halting wedding walk. Your mind removes the wedding dress. You are unable to name the parts of the body. You attempt to recover past pleasures with mnemonic details: where you met, what was said, her perfume, was it night or day, was it here or Montreal. You imagine the bride as she was beneath you and you are looking into her brown eyes, when suddenly they change and become bright blue with black lashes. Whose eyes? Hers? Was it the summer of your father's death or the summer before Ted was born? It was summer.

You now remember the heat, your bodies wet with love and sweat, sliding against one another all night long, every night. Except week-ends when you went to the cottage. But which summer was with her? And whose blue eyes? There is no more recall. You are alone in your imagination, waiting.

The ceremony is over. You look about, find yourself in the midst of smiling strangers. A wave of excitement comes over you. You decide you are in the prime of life, your hair is still thick, your belly is flat and your arms strong. I will go to the reception. I might even stay in town tonight. But not alone, dear god, not by myself. And if I must lie to Marylou, it must not be for nothing. And should you suspect another woman, Marylou, then you can add martyrdom to your other virtues. Isn't that the only jewel missing from your crown?

The night before his wedding, he dreamed he was in a brightly-lit tiled tunnel. He knew it to be the Hudson River tunnel, although it was empty of traffic. A few yards down to the right a policeman stood on an elevated platform behind a railing. He paid no attention to him. From where he stands in the tunnel, midway between the exits, he can see both exits, which are pitch black. The significance of this dream is obvious, and he decides not to tell his psychiatrist about it.

The reverse trip now. This time the bride has her arm linked through the arm of her (new) husband. Bride and groom must run a gauntlet of consuming stares as they walk rapidly up the aisle, she smiling upon the rows of upturned (avid) faces on her right, he greeting those on his left, as if they had divided the territory by prearrangement. For most it is the first sight they've had of the groom. The deep lines down his cheeks are at variance with his eyes, which are ingenuous as a child's, giving him an appearance of a youth suddenly aged. Bride and groom present happy expressions. They are being photographed by someone facing them at the end of the passage. The flash bulbs pop. One of the pictures will be chosen by the bride for its verity. Their faces, his and hers, will be framed and hung on her mother's wall; taken off her father's wall in Mexico by Raquel; and will hang on their bedroom wall for a period of time at present unknown.

Dreams Judith the man sitting next to her has been drawn to her side by a force beyond his control. As the pew begins to fill up, he presses against her. Actually, it is she who presses against him. He wears a dark blue uniform with gold braid on the sleeve of the arm (pressing) against her (right) arm. His hand, with broad blunt fingers and clean fingernails, is brown skinned. He has been around the world countless times (dreams Judith) but until this moment has not realized that he has been searching for her. She wishes she knew more about uniforms. French? Capitain, mon capitain, c'est moi! Russian, perhaps. If he wants me, he will have to defect. How will we communicate? We will talk with our eyes. One of her big dark eyes, her left, keeps closing in an uncontrollable tic, brought on by excitement. Perhaps he is an American doctor, in the army only to help the wounded. Judith decides a man should not be judged by his uniform. Suppose, though, he is only an airline pilot . . .

Outside a gray stone mansion, the wedding guests stand uncertain: whose house is this? They are looking up at a miniature castle with a turret and spires and a red tiled roof. Before entering, they check their invitation cards. Once inside, however, they are reassured: the austerity was only a facade: the interior has the familiarity of a good hotel. Right inside the door there is a long shiny bar with three tiers of colored bottles. The bartender is greeted like an old friend.

Someone is here who will want to kill herself for love. For love of me. She longs to be enslaved. I shall oblige. I shall be her master. I must be on the qui vive, on the alert, for the signs. She will be neither young nor old. Suicide is a temptation only in the midst of life, not when one is beginning the game of love, nor when it is too late. She will be exuberant or melancholy: there is no compromise with these women. She will talk too much or not at all; her eyes will search but remain empty; she will drink steadily, yet stay sober.

Someone is here who will threaten to slit her wrists or take all the pills or throw herself across subway tracks. I shall dissuade her with kisses. She may have had promises before, but not from me. They will appear different. They always do. Once she trusts me, it will take great skill to get her to the edge of despair without breaking any promises. Timing is of the essence: I must be there to stop her at that final, that exquisite, moment between life and death. I shall rescue her. The thought excites me. I feel a passion greater than I have ever known. Each time I will bring her back to life with my sex. Alive, but in a state of shock, pale, faint, indifferent to what I do with her, I shall take her up tenderly, lay her down gently, and let her have it. She who was at death's door an hour ago, will be screaming with ecstatic pain, wishing she could enter oblivion with my cock inside her.

From then on, I shall drive her to the brink. Again and again. Give, withhold. Declare, deny. Cajole, threaten. Ignore, punish.

But what if I...should...what if I get trapped...nothing is impossible...what if it is she who is out to...and what if I am unable to...

In the reception line the guests await their turn to smile upon the couple. At the sight of the bride's waxen face, their prepared words do not come. It must be assumed that hers is a smile of pleasure, it is her wedding night after all, she is not so young, although her shorn hair makes her look child-like, innocent almost. As a matter of fact it is a startling sight altogether: under a halo of orange blossoms the young-old face, seen for the first time without colour, naked, no artifice anywhere, not around the eyes, nor on the cheeks, the mouth bloodless. The ghostly face with its mysterious smile causes a slight shock, and the wedding guest barely manages to stammer some felicitation and quickly move on. Fortunately, the groom behaves as one would expect. He has a handshake that reaches out, grips, reassures and releases with decent impersonality.

Fred is not obliged to stand in the reception line, but shuffles along in order to speak to the bridesmaid. She is not here. Just the bride and groom. Too late to get out of it. He must say something to the bride. What's all this about forgiveness.

The affair ran its short course that summer. (It was summer.) Watching the bride's radiant smile, Fred notes that she has a sensuous mouth. A sudden recollection of strong white teeth, but not of this wonderful smile. Surely she did smile. Yet he cannot place a smiling face in any frame of the past.

It is a fact: the bride has good teeth. The teeth will remain white and strong for most of her life, so that no matter what befalls her, she will retain her girlish overbite.

— A virgin, a virgin, is there a virgin in the crowd? the mayor shouts.

The bride is halfway up the stairs, leaning over the banister, her bouquet held aloft.

— Come on, come on, if there is one virgin here let her come forward and catch it, ha ha!

The women hang back, their expressions enigmatic. The men are titillated: whisper wisecracks. No one moves. The bride hesitates: what if no one will catch the flowers . . .

Finally Edie speaks: "Now, girls, the term is only a figure of speech. We know, don't we, girls, that virginity is a state of mind." She signals the bride to wait. Goes to the kitchen and comes back with the Widow MacDonald. A proper choice, it is agreed: carnal knowledge is entirely absent from the lady's face.

"My mother looked like that," Mrs. Endicott remarks. "When I got married she told me to recite the thirty-second Psalm, it would help me get through the night, as it did her. 'Blessed is he whose transgression is forgiven, whose sin is covered.'"

The Widow MacDonald knows her place. She obeys orders. She is not perturbed. She steps into what has become a little clearing in the hall, holds out her arms to receive the flowers. Walks smartly back into the kitchen, where she at once places the blooms in a vase with water.

And Leon in the doorway face red breathing rapidly in no shape for three flights of stairs...I make no move he stands there smiling easily that smile I hate unctuous and arrogant yet I am drawn to it drawn to him as to a priest's promise...I guard myself...whatever he wants I will deny it to him but he continues to smile and the smile extends to his eyes I look into his big dark eyes fall into them but cannot touch bottom... suddenly I am afraid he will leave me...terror returns... come in, come in, I urge...

So this is where you have been hiding yourself, he says looking around the crummy attic room bare bulb on a dirty string mattress on the floor looking down at my slept-in shirt and trousers...did I disturb you...no, no, I must have fallen asleep working too hard so busy at the office...he allows me the lie because he knows...

Leon has brought some good grass we smoke lying on the mattress...quietly he tells me about his students a new house he's bought some paintings they have great week-ends...he speaks softly...how it is for men like us understands completely has gone through the same shocks...gradually I feel better happy almost drift off...I know he is kissing me...

Much later, but still in time to see her in her wedding gown, Roland finds the bride. He kisses the pale cheek, then stands back to admire her.

— You look gorgeous, absolutely beautiful, he tells her.

Actually he is shocked at her appearance: the shorn hair, the puffy skin, a little pack of kleenex in the same hand that holds the satin train off the floor. The air of suffering. He gives her a (false) smile. Leans forward to kiss her other cheek, permitting him to hide his surprise. With sincerity, which he can afford, since he will never see her again, Roland says he hopes she will be very happy. And looks deep into her eyes, holding back his final statement, which reminds him, despite himself, of the way he used to hold back the climax in their love-making. She waits for him.

— Good-bye, darling, he sighs.

— So glad you could come, she says.

— It was the least I could do.

— Naturally. You never did more than the least.

Let her have her minor revenge. From now on her little decorator husband will have to cope with her nightlong hysterics. Roland is free. Still, he owes her something.

— I was always honest with you.

— True. You never pretended to love me.

She smiles at him. Again the sense of shock. He has seen that smile before: a battlefield smile of survival. In his bed. Soaking the sheets. With her blood. And smiling. That's what put me off the track. I thought she was laughing at me because

21

she was back in my bed, the night after the final night. She kept fainting: and smiling that ghoulish smile. No doctor. Determined to die in his bed.

Pity. Delayed. Roland knows pity. For the first and only time, he freely hugs her to him. And kisses the top of her head. She rests against his chest. Now they can say farewell, decently, like strangers.

At the far end of the house, in front of the glass wall over-looking the garden, the wedding supper has been set out on a long table with a white damask cloth with red "J" 's in the corners. Except for the tomatoes, all the food is dark: black bread, raw spinach and broccoli, brown rice, black beans. "Not very appetizing," someone suggests. Edie points with pride to four large silver platters, each with an entire cold salmon resting in it. These wondrous specimens appear life-like, silver scales on pink flesh, one naked eye staring out from its viscous fluid.

The bride turns away at the sight of the skeletons. I told her distinctly: no flesh of any living creature.

A young dark man in a white jacket with a red "J" on the right pocket stands behind the buffet table. He leans forward slightly. He shows two gold teeth when he smiles. He brandishes two large silver spoons. As plates are thrust at him, he deftly separates with the two spoons the pink flesh from the salmon's backbone. He serves up the fish in this manner until all the exposed meat from the four platters is gone. Only the heads and tails remain. Then the waiter leaves his position at the back of the table, moves smartly around to the front, and with the same two large spoons, flips each half-consumed fish over. He returns to his position of service behind the table. In a short time, there are left four salmon spines of exquisite symmetry. The triangular heads and glassy eyes and notched tails lie stiff in their silver coffins.

Raquel comes too late to the buffet to get any of the

salmon. It took three ladies miming hunger and its allevia-
tion to persuade her to get up from the floor to go with them
to the table.

— Thank you, said her husband (father of the bride), my wife would be offended if food were brought to her. She is accustomed to serving: I have never seen her eat. —

Raquel holds out her plate with both hands. The three ladies heap it full of beans, thinking to make her feel at home. Raquel laughs a clear, throaty laugh. She hands the plate of beans to her husband and lowers herself gracefully to the floor at his feet.

Now the guests stand in single file waiting to pay their respects to the couple. There's a sportsmanlike patience, as at a line-up for hockey tickets. No pushing, no shoving. Once past the wicket, there's the game to look forward to. The couple stands alone. Her mother is having an attack of asthma upstairs. Her father is here somewhere but no one must know that. The bridesmaid is in the kitchen. The best man has disappeared.

Hilda Erikson, while waiting, has been going over the deposits in her mind's bank account, adding up outrages, friendship flouted, trust betrayed, infidelity. She keeps the account open against a rainy day. So that when it is her turn to congratulate the couple, Hilda hands the bride a fiscal statement:

— Anytime you're ready, you can have Gunnar back.

— That's sweet of you, but I am married now.

— Seriously, he's no use to me, you can have him.

— I don't need Gunnar any more, I'm married now.

— Minor technicality. You'll be doing business again.

To the bridegroom, Hilda says:

— I've known your wife since she was an awkward kid of fifteen, with big teeth and big belly. I saw her through the whole mess, adoption and all, and the thanks I got...!

— Ah, I know who you must be. — The groom's face brightens with recognition. — She has told me all that you did. Your intentions were very kind and we shall always be grateful for that.

Gunnar Erikson bends down to kiss the bride on the forehead.

— Darling, I wish you everything your heart desires. I mean it. Truly. Nothing would make me happier than to see you happy.

Overheard by Hilda. A small shock. To realize he is capable of a tenderness unknown to her. And she walks on, clinging to the (unfamiliar) timbre of her husband's voice. So that, should he ever address her with such intimacy, she would be willing to listen to him again.

In this (former) manor house, where she once administered justice; where husband, children, friends and servants existed in a purgatory ordained by her, the old lady now lies helpless in a small bedroom. She imagines nothing has changed: that the servants are lined up in the morning room awaiting instructions; that cheques are on her desk awaiting her signature; that she will hold court in the library after dinner.

The old lady is banging on her door. She demands to know what that noise is, it sounds like a party is going on. — It's the t.v. downstairs. Now get back to bed. — Throughout the night she hears a door opening and closing. She tries to locate the sound. One of the children must be coming down with something. Not Peter, because he is at school in Pickering. She will take his-her temperature in the morning. He-she may not be able to go to school. She is too tired to get out of bed to find out.

Someone is here who has been longing for the perfect lover. She has had four lovers, none perfect. No one has ever really roused her. She will confess that at no time did she feel anything (averting her eyes) down there. Surely . . . I suggest. No, nothing, she whispers modestly; but, compelled to explain, she tells me how her mind wanders.

— At the most critical moments I mentally plan the dinner, or decide to send a red dress to the cleaners or hold a conversation with my sister.

She searches my eyes, do I understand. Of course . . . and I tell her of my own loneliness.

— Sundays are the worst, I reveal.

— Then what do you do?

— Sometimes I stay in bed all day.

— Alone?

— Books . . .

Conversation is important to these women. That's what they rub themselves up against. They want their minds fucked first.

I tell her I own an original Magritte. She's mad for surrealism. Has she read Breton's Manifesto: I have an early edition: in French. I add, you remind me of Nadja, in your fascinating turn of phrase. She's hooked. And so it goes. It could be ice-fishing. One never knows. One must be prepared. That is the advantage of maturity. Young men don't know that you must patiently deflower their psyche.

At first we will meet in public places only. Concerts, libraries, galleries, lecture halls. Not exactly meet: just be there at the same time, coming and going separately, for she is married. Otherwise I would not be interested. She will leave by herself and carry with her the haunting memory of us two having been in the same place at the same time aware of the other being in the same place at the same time aware of the other being in the same place at...ad infinitum.

Just the same, he will have to be careful. These women, once aroused, demand more and more. They lose their minds. It becomes difficult to get them to think of anything except screwing. All at once he feels his age.

David. If you were to walk in, I would pretend not to know you. I would take my cue, don't I always take my cue? I'm sorry I didn't catch the name. It is repeated. David. I stand here, paralyzed, my eyes on the door. If you were to walk through that door and I could see your face again even at this distance, I would be able to move, to talk and to laugh again.

David who? Permit me to introduce myself. By coincidence my name also is David. You see, there is more than one in the world. But you love only David? Ah well, you will have to find out for yourself.

"Hold my hand darling it will soon be over. Calm now, they must not know, be calm. I love you." The groom tightens his grip as pain causes her to double over. Her eyes close, and open again. "I'm all right now," she whispers.

They're going to bind my breasts. The custodian in white tightens the straps on the straitjacket across my chest. You have enough for triplets, are they painful? You must know you old bitch how I ache: they're gorged: I'd welcome a dog to pull on them. I can feel the warm milk dribble down my ribs. She opens the secluding curtain and three pairs of eyes are turned on me. Full of sympathy. She bustling well that's life so many decent girls who'd give anything to be able to nurse their babies isn't that right girls...

What name is spelled out on her bracelet?

In a voice barely above a whisper,
— Father...
— Ah, my dear child, how wonderful to see you again.
— I recognized you in church.
— You've cut your hair, but I'd know you anywhere.
— Is this your new wife? How old is she?
— Her name is Raquel. About eighteen, I would guess.
— She is ten years younger than I. And she already has a baby.
— You must not compare yourself with her. In Mexico the women mature early. They bloom briefly, oh so briefly, my dear. You have a long life ahead of you.
— She is not much older than when I bloomed briefly. You sent me away. You had my baby taken from me. Yet you married a girl younger than your youngest.
— You mustn't spoil your wedding day with bitterness.
— I wish now you hadn't come to remind me.
— You invited me.
— It was a report, not an invitation, to let you know I found a man willing to marry me. You weren't expected. But you never could resist showing off: look at me, look at my beautiful young wife, look at my beautiful little baby.
— No need for jealousy. You remain my beloved daughter. Circumstances will never change that.
— Forgive me, father. I know you are taking a great risk to be here. I must move on, or people will wonder who you are. And thank you for the lovely shawl. Did Raquel weave it?

— Of course. But I chose the colors. The mauve in the middle is the color of the jacaranda blossoms. Mythology has it that the god Xtacopepatl came to earth one day...

— Save your story for the rest of your children. Just tell Raquel I think the shawl is gorgeous.

He says something in Spanish to Raquel, who looks up with pleasure. The bride bends down, moves aside the rebozo to reveal a wide-eyed baby. She tickles the infant under the chin.

— Look, look, he's smiling at me, the bride exclaims.

The wedding guest from Mexico bounces on his heels. His useless left hand remains in his jacket pocket, giving his stance an air of sophistication. A small crowd attends him and his pretty young Mexican wife, who sits on the floor at his feet. He is the father of the bride, and, more recently, the father of the infant swaddled in its mother's shawl. The little coterie leans forward to catch anything he has to say.

"The mineral springs at Cuatlau have great curative powers. They are also rejuvenating. Once a week regularly I take the baths. Would you believe I'm 53? Yes, I am. No chemicals." Dismissing them with a wave of his good right hand. "Natural food, natural air, natural life, with a shot of penicillin now and again, and the mineral baths regularly. Don't burden the liver. That's the secret."

She is on to something. What does it matter what she suspects to-day. She will be dead and buried within two weeks. Her accusations will go to the grave with her.

The garden dark. No moon, no spotlights. Earlier, in the kitchen for a drink of water, Louis found the switch and extinguished the lights outside. Now he slips out the back door and waits. Not too long.

The two figures embrace. Cloud of breath in the cold air.

"Were you seen?" he asks.

"No. I went upstairs, then down the back stairs. Only one maid in the kitchen; she was too busy."

"Good. We must be clever. No need to make others unhappy."

"Your wife?"

"It's not her fault, she's done her best."

"I'm cold; I'm going in."

"Stay. It's been such a long time." Removes his jacket and puts it around her shoulders.

"Now you will be cold."

"Feel. My face. I'm burning."

A sharp blast of wind from the lake blows away her answer. He tells her what she wants to hear.

Two forms on the frozen ground. Shivering, clutching, gasping. Some satisfaction. His. Too cold to continue anything.

He shakes off his coat. Puts it back on. She snuggles inside it, under his arm.

"When will I see you again?" she asks.

"Darling, first opportunity, I'll call you as soon as I know something. I wish I could change things . . ."

"But...?"
"I'm building a swimming pool."

I am not accustomed to being treated like this. No one has ever dared talk to me this way. Rude, insulting. She calls me Grandma. I am not her grandmother. I shall have to have a talk with Anthony. He will have to find me another maid, this one shows no respect. I am always fair, but I insist on respect. It's Tony's responsibility: he has to look after me: he agreed: the house and everything in it will be his if he takes good care of me. Where is my Coalport china? I want my Waterford crystal. I hate imitations. No one tells the truth any more. Tony. You promised to look after me, ever since you were a little boy, I gave you candy, it was our secret, your mother never knew, I gave you candy and you said, grandma, I will take care of you when I grow up. I never see Tony alone, he always comes in with that woman. What is she doing in my house?

The old lady has been told that the noise is caused by plumbers fixing the kitchen sink. And since time for her is no more, having slipped into infinity shortly after her eightieth birthday, she does not realize that the daily noise of walls crashing, hammers driving, drills screaming, is not of to-day, nor yesterday, but the day before that, and the weeks and months prior to yesterday. Each day dawns automatically, into which she slips with no more awareness than a drugged fish into water. Just as well. She has hallucinations about being mistress of a mansion, of possessing furs and jewels. If she knew her helplessness she would discontinue the habit of waking up. For her, the dangers of the day are dimmed by cataracts. It is only at night that the demons are seen clearly.

But right now, she alternately dozes and wakes, sits upright and falls back. Despite her age, her sense of smell is as sharp and protective as a child's. She bends her head forward. Sniffs around the perimeter of a plastic tray holding flowered turquoise plastic dishes and turquoise plastic cups. Fish! Edie is trying to kill her with rotten fish! The smell alone would make you sick. She puts her nose deeper into the dish, she retches, and, leaning over the edge of the bed as over a railing, she vomits. When she has recovered her breath, she wipes her mouth with the edge of the sheet. Promptly falls asleep again. Spittle runs out of the corner of her mouth. Upon waking, three minutes later, she surveys the tray again. This time she smells bitter almonds. Aha! Poison! It is the icing on the wedding cake. With both hands, she tips the tray so that everything on it, salmon, salad, buttered roll, milk, tea and wedding cake, slide onto the floor, some of it on top of the vomit. Tomorrow Edie will clean up the mess and salvage sufficient food to provide another meal for the old lady, who will get nothing else to eat until she eats what has been picked up from the floor.

Let me tell you Maggie what you achieved by killing your-self...nothing...you killed yourself for nothing for no good reason...did you love him that much or hate him that much what did you have in mind beside your hopeless misery...that Larry would what suffer remorse?...your death gave him a headache he caught cold at the funeral ran a fever...Aileen nursed him she came with her little boy and stayed...Larry who wanted no children an impoverished painter no respon-sibilities is a family man now receives the boy's adoration and stirs it into his coffee...for the sake of your tormented spirit and for mine I paid a visit your surrogate ghost what did I hope to accomplish...obtain a message for you that your death brought a revelation an illumination a love after death...?

Arrived without warning your brother my appearance no surprise not a cloud over the eyes his jesus-mask never cracked he is haunted by nothing...showed me big canvases spoke of exhibitions sales good prices not like the old days...Aileen sat where you used to sit waiting like you for a look...the boy at his feet toy cars on a new rug...so little was asked of you Maggie just to blend into the scenery it seemed so simple... why dear god was it so impossible that you chose to...

Larry to the door it was May beautiful night he said looking up at the stars deep breaths the wind was fresh from the river it was all his the earth the sky the very air...you should have lived has made no difference except to me all alone now...we might have shared a world you and I...no Larrys no Leons no more begging...

Father of the bride says, referring to his (young) wife,
— Let her be. She's fine where she is.
Mrs. Endicott trying to lift the nursing mother off the floor, out of public view, to some privacy upstairs, the bathroom perhaps.
He continues,
— She won't leave me.
— Then you should go out with her, it's not decent, in front of everyone.
— It is decent. It is also a miracle. They're accustomed to nursing their babies anywhere and everywhere, it's natural to them.
— Where she comes from, yes, but you were brought up in this country, where this sort of thing is not done, you know perfectly well. It's up to you to teach her civilized ways.
— My dear lady, I'd as soon interfere with a nursing tigress.
Both now embarrassed, but not by the nursing mother. To avoid looking at each other, they stare down at the exposed breast.
Then the other breast. Soon, relieved of her milk by the eager infant, Raquel snuggles into her corner. She smiles at her baby. Then gazes out into the crowd with curiosity. In quick succession her look of contentment changes to distraction then to uneasiness. Why is there no music at this wedding, no songs, no laughter. No one appears happy. There is only noise, like cats at night. At this precise instant, Raquel comprehends her husband's strange reaction to the nocturnal screams. The

43

entire pueblo laughs at the Inglese's habit of running out in his pyjamas in the middle of the night to chase the cats. Those animal shrieks must frighten him just like the shrieking she hears right now. In one continuous motion, as if lifted by invisible hands, Raquel rises from the floor. She says,

"Llevarme a otra parte. Vamonos."

"Esta no es hora para marcharnos."

"Tengo miedo."

"No hay nada que temer. Aqui estas segura. Sientate en esta silla. Esperame. Regresare cuando sea hora de marcharnos."

Fear has made Raquel disobedient: she does not sit on the chair. Instead, she lowers herself into her corner on the floor and pulls the rebozo over her head, hiding her face.

A tap on the shoulder.

— A quiet corner where we can talk…

The voice familiar: an iron command in a velvet tone. Spence follows the directive out of old habit. Marches ahead to the end of the room, past the bay windows, to the left of which is a brocaded love seat. The other tries to get comfortable against the stiff back, there doesn't seem to be enough space for his long torso, stretches out his legs for support, his heels digging into the thick brown rug. His shoes have rubber soles. Looks up at Spence, a statement ready on his lips. But Spence interrupts the (unspoken) words.

— Back in a minute need a drink how about you?

— No thanks. I'm on duty.

Takes his time, bumping, weaving, as if drunk.

Last person in the world thought I'd ever see again lost weight the crew cut gone the hands clasped at his chest just the same I don't trust him what can he want of me now after all this time…

Spence has returned. Sits against a corner of the small sofa. Crosses a knee. Regards his glass. Speaks without looking up.

— Reports in the paper I didn't expect was caught off guard…

— No cause for alarm. We have the situation under control.

— Leaders apprehended that sort of thing…?

— As usual. You certainly took your time.

— Couldn't help it crowd at the bar…

— As usual. Really surprised you, didn't I? Had to get you into line back there in church.

A hand of the past at his throat. Spence runs a finger around his collar. Loosen the tie that's better.

— Last person in the world I expected to see.

— As usual. Unprepared for the unexpected. I was good, wasn't I?

— You played the part as if to the church ordained. No one would believe you are not a man of god. Your delivery, the quotations, your injunctions to the couple, positively sublime.

— I rather enjoyed this assignment. The air of reverence. Hanging on to my every word. I assure you the marriage is perfectly legal. I've been promoted since I saw you last. My rank permits me to perform ceremonies of all kinds. The collar is my cover to-night. You are not to say anything to anyone; my disguise must remain secret. Watch yourself, take care.

— Yes, I understand. Still, couldn't you, just this once, forget you saw . . .

— I have my orders.

— Are you going to . . .

— Later, not here.

— The poor girl. Even her wedding becomes a trap . . .

— That's what they say about weddings.

I dream of entering a small dark cell. I long to disappear in the depths of a prison the way other men long to lose themselves in a woman. Although I have never broken any laws, I am haunted by this desire to be removed from the world of free men. In my imagination I see a big man, a six-footer, in a sand-colored Balaclava, come up behind me, put a heavy hand on my shoulder and command me to stay where I am. My arms will be pinned behind me and I will be searched for dangerous weapons. He will find only a nail file. "Anthony Hoffman," he will say, "you are under arrest for....." For what? For cowardice possibly. Then he will place handcuffs on my wrists. That moment when the handcuffs click, that moment when I am being rendered helpless, when my life no longer belongs to me, that moment is so exquisite that even in imagination I am overcome with ecstasy. Then I must run to the bathroom where I have an orgasm. Sometimes, when she is not busy, Edie helps me by pretending she is the arresting officer. She has that authoritative manner, offensive to some people, which I admire. So it is not too difficult, in the dark of our bedroom, for me to pretend she is my nemesis. She enters wearing a belted raincoat, speaks the magic words, slips the handcuffs on and leads me away to a corner of the room. The key to the handcuffs is kept in the bathroom, on a shelf of the medicine cabinet.

Edie has done her best for me. She has turned this old house into a prison. When I try to make a break for it, she apprehends me every time. What a relief. Sometimes, when I plan a get-away, I become anxious that this time I will succeed. I think of all sorts of clever ruses: that I am only going to the corner drug-store; or that I need oil for door hinges; or that I have an appointment with the dentist. Fortunately, Edie is always on to me and takes me where I have to go and brings me back. I have tried to explain this to my grandmother: that there is no comfort in freedom; that one's endless decisions lead to endless mistakes; that thieves and murderers lurk everywhere. I have tried to make my grandmother realize how well off she is, in the safety of her own room, having all her needs attended to by Edie and me, instead of by strangers in an institution. Here we have a fellowship, so to speak, of prisoners. Yet, unlike them, we have warmth and bright lights and good food and exciting parties. None of which costs us a penny, as in prison, with the clients paying for all of it. One could say we have the best of both worlds.

— You were right, I shouldn't have...

— I told you...

— Yes, yes, but I had no way of knowing...

— What can you expect of a man who is satisfied to...

— Yet he invited me to their cottage for the week-end: "I want you to meet her, if you know my mother you will understand me," he told me.

— What went wrong?

— The fireflies were late last summer, if you remember, which meant that the mosquitos were still fierce, so we had to stay indoors because he's allergic to insect bites, except when we went out in the boat, and that wasn't for long, he kept insisting we get back: back for lunch or tea or dinner: we were always eating, she was always talking, what a week-end!

— Did you... you and he... did you...?

— How could we... that old bitch... out of the question... and in the boat... embarrassing...

— And since the summer...?

— Saw him twice, but he couldn't stay... between planes...

— What are you going to do?

— If only I could find someone else...

— Here he comes...

Her eyes are moist, her throat aches, she is ready to give way. Let the tears flow. The mother of the bride is going to weep. But for some reason, perhaps because she sits alone, unnoticed, on a hall bench outside the swinging kitchen doors; perhaps because the springs of grief are running dry, the tears will not come. She has removed her shoes, loosened her stays, as it were, dropped her shoulders, handkerchief on the ready, but still she cannot come up with a good cry. She needs a stiff drink to prime the pump. She goes to the bar in stockinged feet, slowly, heavily, past the clusters of wedding guests, looking at no one, deaf to greetings. She need pretend no longer: everyone is audience to her humiliation. How could he do this to her! He had his revenge, what more does he want? She could have him arrested, but there he stands, talking, smiling, as if he had every right to be here. Drink in hand, she walks carefully back to avoid bumping into people who step aside to let her pass. Let them see, have a good look, let them know what it is like to be shamed publicly. She had never exposed him to gossip. Whatever she had done, it was always in private. There were never more than two people involved, herself and one other. Never a breath of scandal. Slumps against the bench. She is ready. There is much to cry about. She is old and fat, while he has remained trim and tall, handsome with grey sideburns against his bronzed cheeks. No wonder: he was released by his crime, freed to father a villageful of babies, while she was left lying between cold sheets. All these years he has been lolling about in the sun while she

had to beg a little warmth from anyone who could spare the time. She starts to cry. If you had only believed me, if you had only accepted my denials, if you had only ignored my lies, we might have gotten at the truth with time...

She rocks back and forth, keening for the dead past.

"A few tears are in order, but you're making a spectacle of yourself. Pull yourself together."

"Who is it, I can't see."

"Kay Endicott, what do you mean you can't see!"

"Oh Auntie Kay, I didn't recognize you, I can't see for crying."

"You should be happy she's married. She won't cause you any more trouble."

"You've never had children: you have no right to say that."

"On the contrary. Not having children gives me the right to judge those who have committed the crime of procreation."

"I love all my children equally."

"If you're so full of mother's milk how can you ignore that poor Mexican girl? After all, she is a mother too."

"What would you have me do, kiss her? He only brought her here to humiliate me."

"That's not her fault: you might show a little friendliness."

"I can't bear to look at her."

"It is your duty."

"I've done my duty. I raised his five children, all alone."

"Oh come now. You had help. From the most unusual quarters, I must say."

"I never question from whence comes my help."

"Then be generous. Speak to her."

"What good would that do?"

"It would make her feel better. We were brought up to be kind to foreigners."

"But not to marry them."

"You're not married to her. Your husband is. When he married her in Mexico, he was the foreigner."

"Then I should be nice to him."

"Not in Toronto. For heaven's sake, stop pretending to be stupid. You have to be nice to everyone at your daughter's wedding, regardless of their origin."

Silence.

"I saw their baby, it looks like your Paul did when he was an infant, except for the skin and the eyes and the hair. Come now, you're a mother, as you keep reminding me, wouldn't you like to see the darling baby?"

The weeping begins afresh.

"What's the matter now?"

"Paul is hitchhiking to Mexico to find his father."

Where did all these people come from? Half the city must be here, crowding the walls, standing, sitting, leaning, slouching. There is no partition, no door anywhere, to separate the wedding guests from one another. Round and round they go, around the bar, around the bride, around the groom, around one another, less and less faithful to an orbit with every drink, until the movements become abrupt. Something propels them closer and closer to one another, only to be repulsed by the (dangerous) proximity.

The bridegroom is meeting most of the guests for the first time. He is exhilarated. He goes from one to the other, shaking hands. If they do not come to him, he seeks them out. Sometimes the drink in his other hand spills over a little.

— Sácame de aquí, — Raquel is saying. She is no longer sitting on the floor, and stands slightly behind her husband, so that her words are spoken close to his ear. — Tengo miedo. Tu otra mujer, acquilla, me da mals suerte. Fijate cómo me mira. Algo malo va a courrir, lo sé, lo siento, es su odio, me hace temblar. —

— Stop your foolish tongue. You're as superstitious as your grandmother. There is no such thing as the evil eye. —

— Esposo mio, estas equivocado. Se puede enfermer de odio, incluso te puede mater. Debo marcharme. Ahora mismo. Por favor, antes de que se me agrie la leche y haga enfermer el niño. —

— She is an old woman. Look at her. She cannot harm anyone now. —

— Los viejos son los peores. Tiensen la fuerza del toro a punto de morir. No quiero mirarla. —

Raquel turning her back on the room, face close to the wall, tightens the rebozo, flinging the loose end high over her shoulder. Fingers the crucifix at her throat, presses the silver against the infant's (hidden) forehead.

Father of the bride (and husband to Raquel) now turns to his right, towards Mrs. Endicott, who is all smiles and speaks words of common usage, being words he can understand:

— Lovely wedding, your daughter makes a lovely bride, you don't remember me, but I remember you very well, you used to come to my Sunday school class to pick up your little girls. — She is mistaken, since he would never permit his wife (wives) and children to attend church.—And so this is your new family, how interesting, and is the baby dark or fair, not that it matters, I'm sure you love it just the same, dark babies are so cute with their big black eyes, may I see, my dear— Moving past the husband, behind Raquel and pulling at the folds of the shawl. Abruptly Raquel draws away, quickly hiding her baby, and darts behind her husband, who moves aside, and pushes her forward, exposing her.

— She has never been out of her village, she's not accustomed to strangers, he explains.

Deliberately, relentlessly, he and Mrs. Endicott, with their twenty fingers, together tear the cloth away, to reveal the slit-eyed flat-boned brown-skinned descendant of the Aztecs. The baby twists his head from side to side to escape the glare of light. Raquel prays to the Virgin Mary.

— I do believe, Mrs. Endicott remarks, that anglo-saxon genes are recessive. —

Spencer Reilly. Spence. So little was asked of you. Simply to offer up the toast to the bride. A mere formality. All you had to do was read a prepared paper, the text of which you yourself created, writing it over and over until the words rang sincere. You even taped it and listened to yourself with satisfaction. You made reference to her charm and beauty, her intelligence and sympathy. Not so long ago you believed her to be the possessor of such virtues. Yet, just now, you could not bring yourself to say so. Why? You agreed to be the best man. Delighted, you said, with relief that you were off the hook. Anything, I'd do anything for you… Across her face you saw the familiar appeal: the forlorn waif, the little match girl freezing in a cold, cruel world. You were not taken in: you recognized it for what it was: a calculated innocence: she didn't know anyone whom she could depend upon to make the toast. Overflowing with good will you consented: you just want her to be happy.

What happened to your exuberance? Oh come now. You didn't have that much to drink. You always could hold your liquor. That's how you got where you did. You are able to keep your wits about you when others lose theirs. Even now, sprawled on a chair, your head on your chest, eyes closed, arms loose — even now, you could dispense with the crumpled sheets of paper in your pocket and extemporise a decent tribute to the bride. You're used to making speeches. We were quite willing to join you in what is, after all, a routine. And yet you stood before us, unable to let a few kind words cross your lips. Holding your typewritten pages up to your face with a hand that trembled.

Perhaps your inebriation is not a pretense. It is said "in vino veritas." Is that what happened? You could not bring yourself to lie...

Retraces the childhood steps.

Awkwardly, with his big empty hands hanging inches below the stiff white cuffs.

Speaks the words rehearsed in the dark.

— Father, you must be told the truth.

— I've had more than my share of truths. Please, no more...

— The truth is, father, you deceived me. You told me, write out everything that happens during the week while I'm away and we will talk when I come home. You bought me little spiral note-books and a ball-point pen. You said not to bother her, Mother is too busy. Show it to me only, you said. Every Saturday morning I would bring you coffee and wait at the foot of your bed with the little book in my hand. You drank your coffee, then read the daily entries. You corrected the spelling. The more I wrote the better you liked it. The truth is, father, you had me spy on my mother!

This man regards me like the stranger I am, his face comes closer, showing a (false?) concern.

— Amazing how children misinterpret one's best intentions. What did you do with the notebooks? They would make an interesting document of your childhood.

— After the accident I burned them. In the back yard, along with snapshots you were in.

— My books...?

— No, mother wouldn't allow me to touch them. She still has all your books.

— I'm glad of that. I wouldn't want you to be a burner of books.

Searches the sun-baked eyes.

— Are you telling me the truth?

— I would not lie to you, son.

Thomas' feet are stuck as if in hot tar.

— Take me with you!

— My plans are made, I dare not change them. But I will get word to you and someday you can join me.

Happy now.

Back to dreams of going to see his father, the sight of whom (briefly) woke him.

And the father of his dreams henceforth will have a different face.

Exchange of glances.

Voices rise. The older guests, who don't hear very well, shout. Everywhere one turns there is a mouth open. Aghast. The best man is unworthy of his calling. Speculation rife. Stories circulate. Slowly brought to a stutter by the persistent ringing of a bell. At first the ringing is mistaken for a household bell, a telephone, or the front door. Everyone shaking his head to empty it of the bell, but the ringing continues. Finally, with reluctance, for the rumors have barely begun, they follow the sound to its source. A shepherd's bell, Greek perhaps, is being waved above his head by the mayor.

"Ladies and Gentlemen, it has become my unexpected pleasure to propose a toast to the bride."

The mayor stands in front of the bay windows. White velvet drapes create a backdrop for his iridescent blue silk suit. When he stops ringing his bell, the guests become noisy again. When he resumes, he gets their attention. If he wishes to speak, he must stop ringing the bell. If he does that, he is prevented from speaking by chatter. But he is a politician. He is sensitive to the temper of the crowd. He holds up the wedding invitation, on the back of which is some writing.

"... and I say, if there is anyone else who cannot bring himself to forgive and forget, and who can not, in all conscience, join me in a toast to the bride, you are free to leave ..."

He's got 'em! All eyes front. Everyone rooted with curiosity: who will expose himself?

Now looking at Gerard Broussin. In view of his recent behaviour, he should be the first to declare himself. Instead, he is a spectator like the rest. His face is without rancor. Surely there are others who...

Edie forward, one arm outstretched, palm up, as if offering absolution.

Dr. Peter Fountain walks towards the white arm, eyes fixed upon it. Followed by Judge and Mrs. Everett Ames, and Mrs. Endicott.

Conclusions are drawn.

Resolutely they march, single file, led by Edie. As they pass the mayor he has a smile and a nod for each one. The onlookers separate to make an aisle for the little procession as it goes down the length of the reception room, into the dining room, past the buffet table, where the uniformed waiter regards them with astonishment.

And a choked voice, unmistakably the bride's, please, please...forgive...forgive...

Only those who received an invitation similar to the one still being held aloft by the mayor, with her writing on the back, know why the bride is so visibly disturbed.

HELEN WEINZWEIG

How can I forgive you for what I will never know again. On your knees you promised. Those endless kisses. I was drugged like any addict. Enveloped in your languor. Aware of nothing but your whispers in the night. Now I'm thrust into the light and my eyes hurt from the glare. I do not wish your happiness. After all. It suits me to appear drunk.

62

"You tell 'em, kiddo, they'd better get their feet out of my grave, I'm not dead yet."

All eyes. It is the old lady, who stands beside the mayor, as if dropped from above, one hand in camaraderie on the mayor's shoulder, the other holding a fistful of nightgown, her bare feet tagged like a pigeon's and her short white hair upright in wintry stubs on the landscape of her scalp. The bony head waggles. In the unexpected silence, they think they can hear her skull rattle. It is the click of her false teeth.

Edie glides from the front of the house, towards the old woman, who slips around behind the mayor to his other side. It is an interesting diversion and the guests murmur with amusement. That Edie, so inventive, so original.

The old lady screeches, "That's her, that's the one, help, she's poisoning me!"

Edie has her by the arm. "Come along, grandma, you're dreaming again."

"It's a lie, I only dream in Chinese. Help, she's going to kill me!"

Laughter and applause. Edie raises a hand to halt the sounds of appreciation. The last movement has yet to be played. As if on cue, the old lady runs towards the bride. Twisted fingers poke into the bride's cheeks.

"Are you my lovely Elizabeth come to see your mama?"

She is easily carried off, lifted under her bird's wings by Edie and Tony. On the third step, the old woman recognizes her grandson, pulls away for an instant, raises an imperious hand.

"Anthony, tell her to let go of me, she's hurting me, who is she anyway, she doesn't belong here, I want her dismissed immediately."

"That's Edie, grandma, she takes care of you, she looks after me too, and the house and everything, she's wonderful."

"Sure, grandma, I take good care of you, I bought you the pretty nightie you're wearing. If you're a good girl and do as you're told, I'll buy you some nice blue slippers to match."

Is there no one left who will listen to me . . . there was a time they had to pay attention when I spoke . . . something is wrong . . . where is everyone . . .

"I didn't get any of the bubbly," the old lady complains.

In bed, on her back, arms under the covers, exhausted. Comforted by the familiar stench in the airless room, she falls asleep. And dreams of being dressed in turquoise silk, climbing the steps of a Chinese temple, its green-gold roof and turquoise spire sparkling in the sun. Chimes and gongs and murmuring voices. Small brown figures everywhere. I must be careful, I am the only white person here. All the others are Chinese. There are people who cannot tell one Chinese person from another, but I can. My problem is that I do not recognize any one in my own house. But here in China I know every-thing, I'm not sure what, but it is everything. I feel young, I have my life ahead of me, I will do things differently. Inside the temple, despite the dimness, she heads straight towards the large turquoise urn, into which she deposits a bundle of love letters. A priest bows to her and she bows in return. They smile and bow to one another for a long time. A glow fills her (now young) body with pure love for him. Then she is outside again, in a rocky landscape reminiscent of Muskoka. She can hear water running.

She wakes. Trembles. Someone is in her bathroom. Get out of my toilet! It's mine, don't you dare do your business in my toilet, do you hear!

If the wedding had taken place on Friday, I could not have attended. I do not go out on Monday, Wednesday or Friday. If an opportunity arises for me to participate in a social situation, I will do so only on Tuesday, Thursday or Saturday. These are the uneven days, as propitious as the numbers 3, 7 or 11. Note the portentous letter "u" in the trilogy. What anticipation there is in going to the theatre on Thursday; what excitement in the prospect of dinner on Tuesday; and the joy of a wedding party, as experienced tonight, Saturday. The other days bode no good. After all, what can I expect of a Monday that smells of washing; or a Wednesday, when one must eat the last of the leftovers; and Friday with its uneasy pall, when I can hardly wait to leave work early in anticipation of an eventful week-end. Which brings me to Sunday, to a veritable bonus of choices. On that day I can, with a clear conscience, make irrevocable decisions: whether to stay or go, whether to lie idly about the house or take up a paint brush. This is the open-ended day of total freedom. However, like all exercise of free will, the Sunday decision is fraught with danger. In these times of changing values, when all guide posts are rotted, when all restrictions on decent behaviour are flouted, one must find one's own modus vivendi. On Sunday one must stand up and be counted. But I digress. I merely wished to say that because the wedding is today, Saturday, I am here.

And since I am here, I shall make my unique offering to this auspicious event. In my own modest way I had already made a substantial contribution by persuading her to get married.

"It doesn't matter who you get," I told her, "so long as you have a husband. You simply cannot afford another scandal. Later, when things quiet down, you can review your situation." Before long, a wedding invitation came in the mail. "Thank goodness," Hilda said cryptically. And now, as I observe the bride, and see with what sincerity she moves among her guests, outstanding in her exquisite paleness, I am reassured my advice was correct. Still it is not enough that I be pleased with the marriage. It is important that she have the full support of all her friends, otherwise a poltergeist of hypocrisy would hover around the wedding presents. Not that I am superstitious, but I do feel that gifts begrudgingly given are dangerous to the recipient. The crystal shatters in the sink, the electric appliances burn out, the carving knife will slice a finger. Although I have a good understanding of the forces at work in mine and others' lives, there are times when it does no harm to have one's opinions confirmed. Some sixth sense prepared me for such an eventuality. In my pocket is a packet of papers, on which the question reads, "Do you think I was right to urge her to get married? Circle one only, Yes—No." As unobtrusively as possible, I pass the slips around to certain friends.

I take up a strategic position at the far end of the dining room, near the windows at the back, where I have a full view of everyone and am at the same time readily accessible. One by one the slips of paper come back to me. I am shocked. Only two of the answers are a straightforward Yes. With total disregard for my instructions, the most scurrilous remarks are written on the rest. Decency forbids me to repeat them. Louis tears up his paper before my eyes and remarks that at last she got herself a guy her own age. Is he referring to me? My own thoughts towards the girl were always the purest. My marriage is sacred.

In view of these unexpected reactions, and despite the fact it is my good day, I begin to doubt my judgment. I feel apprehensive. What if I have made a mistake? I had been so interested, that is to say, concerned, about the bride, I never gave a thought to the groom. Silently now I study him as he walks about. I had never met him before to-night. A little too graceful, I reflect, yet something attractive about his light step. I try to fathom his character, attempt to determine what manner of man he is, but he is not giving off any kind of aura I can grasp. All I receive is the outline of his tuxedo with bell-bottom trousers. His moustache is nicely trimmed. His smile is constant, and while he wears a good-humored expression, I have a premonition he would not laugh at my witticisms.

At exactly 9:12 a horrible thought strikes me. What does the bride know about the groom? What has he told her? For that matter, has she told him everything? What do they know about one another? My mind boggles. It is too much for me. I go to the bar. It is, after all, Saturday, and I may get drunk with impunity. Tomorrow is Sunday.

And the champagne has gone flat. A glass is raised.

— Yes, of course, — the mayor is quick to respond to the signal, — we could all use a drink. Waiter, another round of champagne.

— Now then. I presume that those who have chosen to remain will join me in a toast to the bride and give her our blessings. The bride herself, just a few minutes ago, asked me to take over. Uncle George, she told me, it really doesn't matter what you say, just give me your blessings. I agree marriage should indeed be blessed. But before we give our benediction, let me say a few words about today's bride.

I wish I could begin by telling you how well I know the beautiful young lady, but unfortunately my civic responsibilities have denied me that pleasure. Perhaps I should invent little stories, as is the custom, about her childhood, braces on her teeth, school prizes, or dyeing her hair at thirteen, as my daughter did; little anecdotes that would draw a picture of a normal, healthy girlhood — but to be honest, I have not seen her since she was a very young child. It was her mother I knew very well. The little cottage still stands behind the court house where I'd slip in and relax. In those days the bride was about four years old. When time permitted, I would first go into Woolworth's and buy the child a toy, but all she ever wanted was Silly Putty. She was a good little girl and played in her room until I unlocked the door and let her out. She never cried. As a matter of fact, she rarely spoke.

On a day like this let us stop and reflect upon the mystical union of a man and a woman. I well recall when I got married the war was still on. Although I was not in uniform, I did my duty. I kept physically fit, exercising as diligently as any soldier. In those days there was a shortage of lawyers, but I turned away no one from my office door. I tried in my own humble way to balance the scales of justice. I didn't seek gain yet wealth came. In time, I was persuaded to run for public office. I sacrificed my private life in order to swim with the political tide. Simple pleasures had to be renounced. My family is understanding and write me regularly wherever they happen to be. I always keep in touch. My secretary answers every letter at once. I may be busy, but I am not heartless. It is my civic duty to be available to the citizenry of this city without favor. Tonight, for instance, as much as I would like to relax and renew friendships, I must leave in a few minutes. I am expected at a Kiwanis dinner.

And now, ladies and gentlemen, I ask you to join me in a toast to the bride.

The bride...!

"Where do you live, sir?"

"In Tepoztlan."

"Where exactly is that, sir?"

"South of Mexico City."

"Very interesting. And what exactly do you do there, sir?"

"Anything that comes to hand, in a manner of speaking. But why do you call me sir?"

"No offense intended, a habit of mine from C.O.T.C. days. Permit me to introduce myself, mayor of this fair city, Howard Perkins is the name. I knew you a long time ago, or, more precisely, I knew about you, that is to say, I knew who you were, your picture was on the sideboard in the dining room, before you left the country."

"I see. You were one of them."

"Yes. But that is no longer the issue. You've begun a new life; and I, I no longer enjoy the luxury of a private one. My days are like the pages of an open book. We begin where we are, I always say. Forgive and forget. Right?"

"I wish it were that simple. Who does the forgiving? And forget what? I have no control over my memory. I have no idea why I forget some things and remember others. The importance of the event has no bearing on whether it will be recalled. What is the significance of jam sandwiches eaten in the back yard, or a gallon of white paint won in a raffle? I have forgotten the name of the teacher on whose account I left school at 15. Yet I can remember the exact instance when I saw my bicycle rack empty in the school yard when I was 10. I can still feel the shock, the loss.

"One must take the good with the bad. I lost my Mickey Mouse watch when I was lad."

"How strange that childhood is readily remembered. Yet the most dramatic, the most decisive events of our lives pass into oblivion as if they had never taken place. My mind tells me I lived in this city for twenty years, that I had a wife, a job, home and children. I recall none of it. Even seeing my eldest daughter to-day brought only a swift, fleeting vision of her tiny face at the window one winter's evening. It was a quarter to eight, I was late. That's all. The rest is a vague feeling of time having passed, just as one is aware of a ship having moved beyond the horizon because it is no longer there when you look again."

"You must not upset yourself about such small matters. The human brain is being exposed every day."

"No, the mystery will remain. No one can know which pain will be remembered, which pleasure forgotten. I killed a man, yet I can't recall his face. Only his black leather gloves on the hall table beside my mail: a telephone bill, a circular from Pergamon Press, and a letter from my aunt, which I opened and read right away. It was to tell me my cousin Enid had another boy, her fourth. And the two black gloves slightly inflated, as if his hands were still in them."

"I'm against violence, personal violence, I should say. War is something else. What is your opinion of the political climate in Mexico, do you think the government is stable?"

"Politics don't interest me. I don't want any trouble. I lead a pleasant life in Tepoztlan. A large cool house, flowers, trees, swimming pool, servants. I merely have to administer a simple situation: food and shelter are the only issues."

"Doesn't it bore you sometimes, this peaceful existence? A man of your background, your education, training, in the prime of life, without a challenge. A man needs a challenge. Other than your little muchacha, if you don't mind my saying so. Siestas and sitting about. What happens to a man's character without a challenge? I'll tell you. He gets weak, loses his manhood. Do you know, I have given blood 106 times! That shows character."

"I read a lot. Spanish as well as English. Everything in print I can get hold of."

"You're the man we're looking for, who can read the fine print. Trade commission looking for contacts. Must be trustworthy. The Syndicate follows up. Hemispheric Unity from the Yukon to Peru. Extend the frontiers. Trade is the lifeblood, money is the transfusion."

"But I know nothing of commerce."

"So long as you know their language. The important thing is that you are one of us. We can depend on you. The Syndicate will handle the rest. Oh, you need not worry, we are not crude robber barons. We have a Cultural Division. We overlook nothing. Cultural exchanges to smooth the way, sending the priests ahead, you might say, of music and dance and literature. Scientific exchange too. We could, for example, put a band of our Indians into one of your native villages and have your backward groups come to live on one of our Indian reservations. Interesting sociological study on cross-cultural adaptation."

"There is the problem of influence. I'm not very important in Mexico."

"You leave that to us. Money buys all the influence necessary. If we play our cards right, we will all get a piece of the action."

The two men fall silent.

The mayor, who enjoys a degree of power, suddenly gets a vision of a thousand and one delights. Of pleasures so sublime they are exquisite torture. He may be thinking of secret drugs and sacred rites, or vice versa. Fantasies of being (temporarily) a willing prisoner in a ruined temple, blinded by a strange light, or conversely, blinded by stygian dark.

And the father of the bride, who is indifferent to what the mayor dreams about, conjures a vision of power. Without limit. Power over his mother-in-law, the gardener, the bank, the President himself. Everyone will bow and call him Dottore in the zocalo. No one will dare arrest him.

You can get used to anything, even leg irons.

The old lady tugs at the plastic bands around her ankles. They are identification bracelets, the kind used in hospitals. Regularly she claws at the bands, her fingers searching to undo the loop, but the anklet is held together with wire staples. The skin is always inflamed around her ankles and sometimes the skin breaks and there is blood. Edie will not remove the bands. "I don't care if you bleed to death, they're on for your own good, the way you wander around." The blue lettering on the white plastic reads, on one: I am Diabetic, 120 Rosecrown; and on the other, Call 334-8129. Reward.

— I will hate you as long as I live.

On her moribund lips the words are a mere figure of speech. Love, hate, blame or gratitude: it is all the same to him, he is a doctor, after all, and does what he has been trained to do.

Going upstairs, he stays close to the wall, avoids confrontation and all those meaningless mewings of sympathy. As if he were an ordinary man instead of a doctor! What is he going to do with her clothes? Cupboards full of dresses and coats and shoes, drawers and boxes full of all sorts of garments. The more weight she lost, the more she bought. — No point in saving money now, is there darling? Several sizes here, from a fourteen to a seven, I'm exactly half the size I used to be. The next one can have her choice. You'll save on her clothes. — But she is wrong. There will be no next one. I will go away as soon as it's over, far away, to Venezuela perhaps, for a long time, five-six years, I will do research, I need no more money, I will give my services to humanity, I will lose myself in my work. But what will I come back to? I shall give my house to the bride for a wedding present, I owe her something. Provided I can stay with them on my return. He feels no jealousy towards the groom. For obvious reasons. The three of them would live together. In his house.

The doctor finds his coat in one of the bedrooms, but must go into another room for Doris's. He hesitates in the hall. Women. They never shut a door, always chattering, waving their hands. He goes in. The women become silent. They know what he's come for: they point to twin beds with coats piled. Critical eyes are upon him as he begins the search for his wife's mink coat, the beige one. How tired he is. So many women, so many breasts and buttocks and open mouths, all requiring attention. Yet when you put a hand on them, their bodies dehydrate and float belly up away from him. Luckily he soon finds the mink and buries his face in the fur as he escapes. Voices rise up again as soon as he steps out into the hall, but he cannot hear what is being bruited about.

— That's the man, the doctor. His wife is supposed to die on the 30th.

— What's to-day?

— The 18th.

— What if she doesn't?

— Oh, but she will, he is a doctor.

— Suppose she rallies, they do sometimes, you know.

— Impossible — they say he treats his rats badly.

— Which one is his wife?

— The one with the sores.

— Did you know her when she was alive?

— Yes, she is a pretty little thing, rather pathetic, always begging you to like her.

— Beggars can't be choosers.

— Doesn't she know that?

— Apparently not, or she would have chosen life.

Insists always, even if he is forced to shout, that he is a man who speaks his mind. Thomas. In contrast to his upright manner, that is to say, a bluntness of speech he mistakes for rectitude, Thomas's shoulders are hunched, his back is rounded, his head droops. He looks out from under his brows with belligerence, ready to back up his honesty should it be challenged by a candor equally naked. Thomas is not certain his sister's intentions are honorable, but, having expressed his opinion unequivocally, he agreed, for sentimental reasons and because their father is a fugitive, to give the bride away. At this moment he sits on the striped sofa trying to decide whether it is more honest to face his father now in front of everyone, or follow him later to wherever he is staying and tell him the truth privately.

A young woman in a short skirt and purple stockings has seated herself next to him.

— Are you related to the bride or the groom, she asks.

— The bride, Thomas replies without hesitation.

— You're not her brother Thomas!

— Yes, and I'm not ashamed to admit it.

— My name is Luba, I'm an old friend of your sister's.

— You're making it up.

— No. Honestly. We were in high school together.

— She went to high school for only one year. My sister had no girl-friends.

— But it's true, honest.

— She only had boy friends. I can't trust you.

— I was only trying to . . . Wait, where are you going?

— I must speak to my father. Right away. It is my duty.

— Oh, how forthright you are! I admire a man who is sincere.

— Do you really? Not many people appreciate sincerity.

— Sincerity is so honest!

— Then you don't think my honesty is foolish?

— On the contrary. It takes a special mind to be perfectly honest.

Her perfume is convincing, but he must not be corrupted by externals. Thomas tests her:

— If you were my sister's friend, how is it we never met?

— She made me promise to keep her visits to our house a secret. We are Ukrainian.

— True. We led a circumspect life.

— The bride, your sister, loved music. My father would play the accordian, sing folk songs for hours. He was unemployed.

— My sister refuses to listen to music, you're making it up.

— Figure it out, that's why she hates music now, because she loved the music my father played for her. The association, don't you see? The music, my father, the abortion, it's all tied together.

The truth of her statement overpowers him.

— What about your father, what happened to him, did he continue to play the accordion and sing?

— He has never stopped. There's always someone willing to listen.

— I find that commendable. It's consistent. My father had no talent, and I must tell him so.

— There's an old Ukrainian proverb: truth on an empty stomach is like lipstick on a corpse. Why don't you eat first?

Thomas realizes he is hungry.

— I see now why my sister liked your house.

Together they approach the buffet. He holds the plates.

She goes from dish to dish, lifts the serving spoons, only to put them back again, empty.

— I think I'll just have some black bread.

— My sister has become a vegetarian.

— There's an old Ukrainian proverb that says those who do not eat meat devour one another.

They have been led to a room beyond the dining room. Edie half turned around in the doorway, saying the bartender will look after them. She will be back to let them know when it is safe to come out. Shutting the door behind her.

The two men and two women in a small circle in the middle of the room. A surprised silence. Thrown (unexpectedly) together by a common intransigence.

I didn't know anyone else feels as I do...

A cold pervades. Mrs. Endicott's hands on the (warm) radiator. Looking about, thinks, I have been here before: they say it is an effect caused by a time lag between the optic nerve and the brain. A small sitting room, cluttered, crowded with overstuffed furniture. On the walls reproving faces in thick oval frames arouse guilt. Tea things of long ago on a brass table. It is all so familiar, including the overtones of guilt. Mrs. Endicott finds a chair she knows is going to prove uncomfortable. Pulls up a petit-point foot stool.

Judge Everett Ames is seated at a walnut desk. He fingers the brass lid of an inkwell, peering into it at the crackled ink inside. With subliminal sight also sees his wife move cautiously towards the door. As she puts her hand on the knob he says flatly, without raising his head, you will stay right here.

She letting go of the knob. I missed my chance. Again. To walk out on him. Whereupon Mrs. Ames sets her expression into (habitual) submission, retreats to a corner opens a small silk purse and fills her mouth with five sticks of gum, one after the other, the entire package. Chews fiercely, lips compressed.

Dry sound of wood against wood. The judge rapping an old pen against the edge of the desk. Not to be compared with a gavel, yet attention is drawn. All at once he is at ease. Contemplates the upturned faces, serious and concerned, looking, he thinks, to him for a verdict.

— It is better to be conspicuously absent than to bear false witness. There are many out there who are at this moment pretending to forgive her, they drink toasts to her happy future, all the while harboring ill will. We are sequestered here because we refuse to be hypocrites.

Mrs. Endicott digs broad, flat heels into the footstool.

— I don't know what you are talking about. I'm here because my feet hurt. I have nothing against the bride.

The doctor notes her ankles are puffy.

— And you, Dr. Fountain? What brought you in here?

Who is checking his own pulse. It's racing again, at the sound of my name. Reflexes, simple atavistic reflexes brought me into this room. Danger. My heart. Fibrillating.

— I was her doctor. It's a classic case: she was all alone, the big city, helpless, in pain. She would telephone me at all hours of the night. I couldn't get any sleep. If I put her off, I still couldn't sleep: visions of her lying there in pain. It was no use. I learned to simply drag myself out of bed and go to her. How can I ever repay you, she kept asking.

— All alone — the judge repeats, — father gone, mother uncaring. Thousands like her passed through my court. I'll never understand myself. It's alright, my wife knows everything. She stood by me throughout the scandal.

— Gave up my practice. Three years in Frobisher Bay. I exhausted myself daily. Slept well.

— It was an impression you received. I've known the bride all my life and I can tell you she never left home: she never was alone.

— I thought it was a rooming house. It looked like a rooming house. At that hour of the night. I always left before anyone wakened.

— Who would not have come to her aid...Yes...All the time one thinks one is in a strong position...everywhere I went I was called Your Honor...then one mistake...and down, down, down...

Mrs. Ames removes her wad of gum with a delicate gesture and places it in an ashtray, which, strangely, is full of old cigar butts.

— My life is unchanged, she confides to the other woman.

Where is the bartender, we are being neglected.

I have been travelling a long time. From one strange place to another, from one dirty, ugly city to another. In the plane I look down on painted patches on a painted landscape. Nothing moves. I cannot even guess at the lives I know are being lived out down there behind the brushstrokes. And I, travelling on behalf of those invisible creatures, with a black leather case heavy with the facts of their existence, am, in turn, invisible to them. We will never meet.

And when my feet touch ground, I am unable to distinguish the language spoken around me. I talk to no one. I make signs for my needs: a room, food, a taxi. Only the next flight saves me from disappearing altogether. I rush to the airport and get there hours ahead of time. I've escaped again. The loudspeaker clicks. The channel opens. Welcome aboard, the captain says.

Well, I tried. She's wrong: her brother is not what she thinks he is. There he goes peddling truth, solemn as a missionary. O lord, prays Luba, find me a man with a sense of humour.

... roared with laughter when we got tangled in the sheets...

Dreams Luba that somewhere in this world is a man who has been searching for her all his life. Faces of men standing about in small groups. Their women are elsewhere. The men are concentrating on one another, heads inclined, arms rigid. Intent on trade? Imagines herself going up to one of them, the one with the reddish hair, for instance, removes all her clothes, one by one, take me, take me, I'm yours... He is annoyed by the intrusion: hesitates for just a moment, then continues... as I was saying...

And the old longing evokes her phantom lover, who floats in behind her wide-open eyes. His features are indistinct, but his ardour is tangible and causes her to tremble.

Suddenly, without warning and without her consent, her lover materializes beside her. He is hunchbacked, dwarfed, a large head straining from humped shoulders towards her. He has the face of a long-suffering saint. And in his beautiful face she recognizes a promise of the marvellous. A deep voice, unlike any other voice she has ever heard, the words riding on a melody.

— Ah, here you are. I've been looking all over for you.

— No, no, you've made a mistake...

— Come, my dear, come, it's time to go home...

A soft beard brushes against her neck.

— Please, I don't wish to hurt your feelings... you've got the wrong person...

— All right, darling, you want to play one of our little games... who do you want to be... Juliet, Isolde, Katherine...

— Katherine...?

— You know... Spencer and Katherine...

— I beg you... go away... see, I have identification... my driver's license... my name is Luba Cherniak, 5'3", eyes hazel, hair dark brown, born... that's me, you've made a mistake...

Gets to her feet. Flight.

— Ah, Gerard, you've come to my wedding! I didn't expect... I sent the invitation because... never for a moment did I think...

— Well, the little card did the trick. I went out of my head... to have lost you... I couldn't bear the thought... finally I did what you had always wanted me to... I said good-bye to my family, my home, my job. I've come to take you back with me.

— My darling, it's too late, I changed my mind while waiting for you to make up yours.

— I have decided. I will wait for you. No need to disturb the party. When you've finished with your masquerade, we will leave together.

— I can't. I'm married.

— No matter. I have paid the rent on the old place and brought my books. I bought six new towels. I threw out his shaving things from the bathroom and his slippers from under the bed.

— Gerard looking at the groom's feet, says, slowly,

— But he can't be the one...

— No. Permit me to introduce my husband.

The two men shake hands.

The groom says, — It's a shame you've come all this way for nothing. Perhaps you'll visit us when we're settled.

Gerard, ignoring him, — My beloved, come with me, these past four months have been hell, I can't go on...

— You surprise me: the boulevardier pleading like a schoolboy. No. No more. Rewards at night and punishments in the

morning. I warned you the last time. There is no profit in me
any more. Go. Go back to your family: they will forgive you.

Looking to her (new) husband. For approval? But he is
watching Gerard in wonder. She, turning towards Gerard to
see the cause of her husband's apprehension, sees her (former)
lover's mouth working as in an epileptic fit.

Who does she think she is this whore in the white gown
unctuous with borrowed respectability making me appear
ridiculous in front of all these yokels who are just waiting to
dip their spoons into my stew . . .

Come now move on whoever you are, we have to pay our
respects, let's get it over with . . .

Other lands, other customs.

Gerard spits in the bride's face.

Everyone watching: one would think it was an act put on
for their entertainment. Not one of the spectators moves to
apprehend the perpetrator of (so heinous) an insult.

The groom takes a handkerchief from his pocket and wipes
the spittle from her cheek.

— It was an accident, he says.

Is that her? Is she the one? That shapeless old woman, is she the one I killed for? About the same height, the same eyes. Yes. I recognize the sea blue eyes. Those eyes that turned me into a mendicant every time. She's older. Of course. Much older. And blonde. Terrible straw hair. It was dark once. I think. Brown or black, but dark. She's fat. I used to be the heavy one, she complained about my weight on top of her. I've changed too, I suppose, the years, the hard work, my gray hair. Does she recognize me? Yes. She's looking straight at me; she knows who I am. I can't recall much else about our life together. There were children running and shouting and my waiting for them to go to bed. And riding home on Friday nights 150 miles from Nobel with five other men, dirty jokes all the way, and handing her the envelope of money. She hangs her head. She's weeping. This, then, is the moment. I don't feel anything. Should I feel some satisfaction? All these years I imagined this moment: I would confront her with my resurrected self and she would know I had escaped her, as I escaped the law. I would look at her and hate her, hate her frankly and openly. I'm going over and tell her exactly what I think of her. Yet I can't move. My mouth is sour. The discomfort is mine. She is a stranger to me, like all the rest. I came all this distance for nothing. There is nothing to be said, nothing to be done.

She looks up at him, her beautiful blue eyes brimming over, just as he makes the (irrevocable?) decision. She seems to know what he's thinking. She lowers her head and begins to sob again. Reaches into her purse she extracts another handkerchief. Her open purse slides to the floor and its contents spill, lipstick and pills rolling along the hall.

...He runs to her. Finds himself on his knees, retrieving the lipstick, the 222's, comb, compact, pen, shopping list, which he reads: javex, grapefruit, polident (she's lost her teeth?) lettuce, tomatoes, butter, wool gloves, t.v. guide. Her mind is as disorganized as ever. "T.V. guide! " he shouts at her, "You're still into your childish escapism, it used to be comic books, and now I suppose you spend all your time watching television!" "My darling," she says, "calm yourself, it's only because I miss you so. Come here. There, isn't that better." He places his head in her lap, she bends over him, strokes his hair, speaking softly into his ear, "If you will come back," she continues, "I promise to read your books, discuss them with you, take long walks to the library. You know I can do it if I put my mind to it. I will hold you in my arms all night. Just say the word and we will begin again. It will be like the old days before the children came." "Tell me about the children, are they here, point them out to me," he asks. "Thomas is here, that's him on the sofa speaking to the girl in purple stockings. He worries about his liver, that's why he's so thin. He studies Sanskrit and eats only brown rice. And of course our eldest daughter, the bride. You see, she's respectable after all and your fears were unfounded." He says, "She takes after you. I mean, she is as beautiful as you were when we got married." "Thank you. Then there's Jenny, she's a novice in a convent. Two more years to go. She's pretty too. She has your small eyes, but they're bright, like her spirit. She's very well liked. Sleeps in a cell next to the Mother Superior." "And the other two boys?" "Yes, tall and handsome like their father. James was the serious one, remember? He's a captain in the American army. I don't know where he is. And Paul, the baby, he's 18 now. He's somewhere too." "Then you're all alone? Or is there —?" "Oh no, I realized that you are the only one for me. There's no one like you in all the world. I will never give up hope that you'll come back to me."

... She looks up at him tearfully just as he makes the (irrevocable?) decision. She always seemed to know what his thoughts were. He watches her fumble for another handkerchief. The open purse slides off her lap, its contents spilling at her feet. But it is no concern of his. What is she to him now? She attempts to pick up the articles off the floor, but cannot bend over far enough to reach them. She continues to cry, rocking back and forth, a sodden hanky in one hand and a dry one in the other. Kay Endicott comes along and retrieves the articles off the floor, replaces them in the purse and snaps it shut. She sits down on the bench beside her. She speaks to her in a persuasive manner. Let Aunty Kay deal with the wretched woman. He's well out of it.

— Do you hear that?

— What?

— That awful laugh.

— It sounds more like a scream.

— Don't look now, but in a moment turn to your right. Doris is raising bloody hell. O.K. now.

— Like wow! What an act! Didn't think she had it in her. She used to stand in corners and make those whiny little sounds. She was always afraid of him. If you're going to make a fuss, I used to tell her, make it worth your while, make it loud and big, like the Slavs or the Sicilians.

— At this stage of her death, what has she got to lose. When you've gone past the point of no return, it is permissible to yell your head off.

— Funny how death has changed her personality. I don't recall ever seeing her so violent, look, she's trying to scratch his face.

— She should have started long ago and not waited until she's dead and almost buried.

— Too bad she's going all at once. I mean, you can die in easy stages, take your time, don't trip over your shroud.

— Exactly. First, she should have had a few years of chronic diseases, bronchitis or a slipped disc or some rheumatism, together with a lapse of memory to avoid confrontations. There are easier ways of outwitting your husband than dying.

— You're right. When I get depressed with those long empty days, each day the same as the one before, I take a few

92

extra sleeping pills, not enough to kill me, just enough to have a good long sleep and scare the hell out of everybody.

— Or you can leave this world in other ways, not necessarily bodily or painfully. There's yoga or television or pot or sex, or a combination of them all.

— At our age it would have to be a little of each.

— You don't have to die to prove your existence.

— All your clothes go to the Salvation Army.

— And the next wife gives your furniture to her poor relatives.

— That's the tradition.

— Thank god for tradition. Otherwise we wouldn't ever know what to do with our worldly goods.

— Tradition is all right as far as it goes, but it can go too far. Suppose you want to be cremated with all your possessions, down to your blender and your cat, then tradition is a nuisance.

— Perhaps I didn't make myself clear: so long as there's tradition, we're free to break it. Do away with the conventions, then everything becomes conventional, even going up in smoke with your pets and your appliances. This way, with marriages and funerals and forks to the left and thank-you notes and daily baths, we have sign-posts to guide us.

— Or we can ignore them.

— At your own risk.

— Everything is.

— What?

— At your own risk.

Now the bride and groom descend the stairs. They look like nightclub twins entering from the wings. The same height, the same gamin haircuts, identical grey suits, red shirts, long beads and melton cloth greatcoats. Black boots with heels. Gratuitous remarks from the audience guests: that's her with the flowers; that's him with the moustache. At a signal from Edie, the couple halts half-way down the steps. That's right, hold his-her waist with one hand, the other on the banister, now, throw the bouquet. To a virgin of course. Hold it! Flash bulbs pop. Smiling upturned faces.

Bride and groom linger at the foot of the stairs. This is the bride's final scene. She waits for the cheers, the good-wishes, the fond farewells, amidst a salvo of confetti and streamers. That is what she has paid for. Instead there is a paralysis. And silence. A boredom is spreading. The bride's mother has stopped blowing her nose. The captain's hand, hidden by the crowd, which has been kneading Judith's right hip, has dropped to his side. Raquel has stopped praying, although she still looks frightened. The bride's father puts back in his pocket photographs of land outside Tepoztlan that does not belong to him. The mayor has trouble breathing. Tony would like to get to bed, if Edie will let him fold and stack the chairs in the morning. Doris, who will die next Saturday, is self-conscious about the missing front tooth (upper) and covers her mouth with her hand. The ebullience of just a few moments ago has given way to impatience. Hurry up, get on with it, let the curtain come down, we've better things to do than stand and watch your act. There are love affairs to be started (ended); there are facts of life (death) to come to terms with; there is wealth (power) to be dreamt about; and there is, all that booze waiting that will give us surcease from love and facts and dreams.

Go on, get going! Edie flings open the front door. Cold sharp air causes heads to turn. Edie stands behind the door, out of the draft, and her voice is as sharp as the wind outside. "Hurry! I can't keep this door open forever, get out!" No choice. The stars exeunt, the heavy door shuts behind them. They are orphaned out on the dark deserted street. At an upstairs window a face (whose?) appears and disappears. They must run to keep warm, which is just as well, as it creates an illusion of eagerness.

Inside the car, the bride trembles. Edie. You bitch. You damned grasping bitch. You promised, I paid you well. Another five minutes was all I needed. There was no proper leave taking: I parted from no one, left without a word, no one kissed me. I touched no one's hand. You robbed me of my final moments.

The groom is concerned, thinks she shivers with cold, drapes a rug across her knees, arranges a scarf over her head, ties it under her chin, tucking the ends inside the collar of her coat.

"I don't want you to catch cold."

"You are so good to me."

She kisses his hands.

A door opens and closes.

. Tradition demands you be thrust out into the cold. Take the first step and you must take all the rest, until you are out of sight. No turning back to warm your hands at the fire. Out, out...

There is a directness about her which appeals to him. Perhaps it is an honesty he is not accustomed to. Fred thinks he is making headway.

— Can I drive you home? Whenever you're ready, just thought if you didn't have...

Anxiety in the voice. Fear of refusal? Something more than a car-ride is at stake.

As he keeps talking Luba recognizes the signs: the leading questions, the eye-to-eye punctuations, his unguarded face, the tension in the legs, the way he rocks on his heels. The glaring moment of his need illumines hers. She knows desire arises spontaneously and unless plucked at its ripeness falls wasted. A worm of a wrong word rots the fruit. Still, she hesitates. She is tempted to take a risk, a long shot, and not give in right away. Some phone calls first, a few dinners, dancing maybe, diversions, dear god, to break the monotony. Yet, if she misses this chance, it could mean a long dreary winter without the sound of a key in the lock. She sighs. In the knowledge she will stay home nights waiting for the call from a phone booth. Then, as she always does when she yields to illusion, Luba puts her face close to his, an intimate touch on his arm, her voice low, yes, he may take her home.

Upstairs, as she pulls her coat out from under a heavy pile, Luba thinks, I should have bought a car. She does not look in the mirror, she does not comb her hair nor put on any lipstick. In the hall, a wraith of an old woman breathes in her face, hissing, — The wages of sin come in a plain brown envelope without a return address.

Downstairs, Fred looks at his wristwatch, the one which will be on Luba's night-table, the hands visible in the dark, and which will time his visits.

He, too, will be compared with David.

— Did they cry during the ceremony?

— Yes, didn't you hear them?

— I was concentrating on the minister.

— Your mother cried all the way through.

— Anyone else?

— Many more, women sobbing and men blowing their noses, especially when he pronounced us man and wife and whom God has joined let no man something asunder.

— That's the nicest part.

— When I kissed you, the crying got quite loud. Did they cry for you or for me or for themselves?

— I think tears are a mark of respect for what is going on. If you don't cry, it's because you don't care. All those people caring, imagine!

— Even if only for a minute.

— It doesn't matter, a deep sigh will do.

— Any response is better than none.

— A laugh or a cry.

— Indifference is unbearable.

— Good to let it out.

— No use holding it back.

— It's been so long...

— Since you cried?

— Yes. I would like to feel some warm salty tears. I cried when Maggie died and Leon cried when I told him you and I were to be married.

— Life can be so sad.

— Do you feel like crying?
— Not now. Maybe in an hour or two.
— It will do you good.
— Music helps. Let's turn on the radio.
— I'll wrap these blankets around you. Now you can relax.

They need not have delayed that extra hour. No one was nosing at the heels of their intent. No one had to be put off the track. The bride and groom were forgotten two minutes after they went out the door. All the parts had been played out: they were on their own the moment they got out of their wedding costumes. And they should have left town for a honeymoon, even a symbolic one: rituals are not to be trifled with.

Upstairs, in the room usually kept locked, the old woman gasps for air. Mixed with the stink of her flatulence is the smell of vomit and fish. Somewhere in the region of her thymus, an alarm goes off. Fear. Fear without knowledge, as in childhood. Straining her eyes and ears. There is a sound, then a shape. She slides under the covers, then peeks out. It is not Edie.

"Who are you?"

"Is there anything I can do?"

"Go away, I don't know you, do I?"

"That makes us even. I don't know who you are either. I was in there and I heard you crying. It's O.K. You're old enough to cry. I was curious, that's all."

"Wait! Come back! Don't step in the mess, over here, closer, come closer. Listen, listen. She is trying to poison me!"

"Sure, sure."

"Wait, wait. I'm telling the truth. There's truth you know even in what I imagine. See, I vomited. The fish was poisoned. It made me bring up, bring up."

"I have to go now."

"Wait. What is your name?"

"Judith."

"Judith. You are well named. Fate brought you here to avenge me. Come back soon. And bring the police. They will arrest her and I will have my house again. It's my house. All of it. I'm rich, I will reward you. You may use my bathroom anytime you want. Promise me, promise, Judith, you will rescue me."

"O.K. grandma —"

"I'm not your grandmother!"

"I'll do what I can."

"Don't think you can humor me. I'm on to you. You're a psychiatrist, you've been sent to find me insane. Then she can get my money as well as everything else. They gave you a key, that's how you got in."

"The door was open, I was looking for the bathroom."

"You're lying. The door is always locked. She's afraid I'll get out and go to the police, she keeps me locked up. Of all people, you, a doctor, swearing oaths. You shouldn't lie. It is a sin to lie. And the wages of sin are subject to inflation: you get less and less value for your sins as time goes on."

"I confess: I have sinned: I have taken the Versailles Room away from the bride."

"What are you talking about! You need a psychiatrist! Versailles is in France. I was there in '28, just before the Crash."

"You're too smart for me, grandma."

"Oh I get up pretty early."

"If virtue is its own reward, do you think evil is its own punishment?"

"Hard to say. It's all a matter of proportion. Small virtues and big evils are always rewarded. But large virtues and small evils should be punished because they're tedious. It's lucky for you you admitted who you are, otherwise I would have put my curse upon you."

"It wouldn't have worked. We Jews have been cursed by experts, beginning with Jehovah. Every curse known to man has already been put upon us."

"So that's why so many of your people become psychiatrists. Trying to figure out why we're so mean to you. I never did anything to you, why do you come here and ask me these personal questions?"

"You can ask me a personal question if you like."

"Are you married?"

"Not yet."

"Getting on, aren't you? I was married at 19 the first time. Have you been in love?"

"Many times."

"And when you fell in love, did you wash his socks?"

"Naturally. And his hair-brush."

"Didn't last, did it? Oh, I know. Women keep making the same mistakes, over and over. Never wash your loved one's socks, or his hair-brush, or iron his trousers. Never handle those items which have touched his skin."

"But I like to, for that very reason."

"You see, my dear, when you change the shape of those articles imbued with his essence, you leech out his virility. Then he leaves you for a woman who handles only perfume and diamonds."

"How clever you are!"

"Let me give you a piece of advice: the next man you meet, don't ask his name. Just weave the gold. Remember Rumpelstiltskin."

"Who's he?"

"Now I'm certain you're a psychiatrist. You have no imagination." Raises her left arm and brings a frail wrist close to her eyes. The wrist is bare. "Your hour is up. And lock the door on your way out."

In the Versailles Room recessed lights cast a sunset glow. An odor of old perfume. Some time soon Edie will install an electronic system to vary the colors and scents. As a result of complaints from clients: vague remarks indicating certain dissatisfactions, which, collated, point to the principle that when stimuli remain constant, pleasures are reduced.

The captain is undressing without haste.

Dread of seeing him without his uniform.

Panic. I have betrayed a friend...never have I...a total stranger...he hasn't said a word...Pulls the sheets up to her chin. The tic in her eye is worse, so that it appears she is winking at him furiously.

Judith observes he is a tidy man: the way he shakes out his jacket before he hangs it up; the rest of his clothes folded neatly on a chair; shiny shoes side by side underneath.

The captain's face and neck are deeply tanned, in contrast to the rest of his body, which is fair, and looks pinkish in this light.

— Pardon, I didn't hear...

— I was just asking why you...

He is beside her, under the covers, caressing her into silence.

Because what he dislikes above all else are the questions. And afterwards, the demands...write me, phone me...It's so much simpler with the ones you pay. Besides, the conversation is less predictable.

"Sorry, darling, I don't know why I cry so much. I'm truly happy you married somebody. The world doesn't change overnight. It's easier for a woman with a husband than without. I ought to know. Even sales clerks write your name with respect if it's Mrs. I never wanted to be without a husband, but the stars decreed otherwise. Life is like that. There I was, one day happily married with five babies and the next day, it seems, they are all gone, husband and babies, gone, all my babies gone."

"Mother, that's history now. Forget it. Your babies are grown men and women. Here's a kleenex. I really must get dressed."

"Oh no matter what you may think, I was aware of my responsibilities. But what could I do, a woman alone. It's all over, I should be enjoying my freedom. Still, how sad. So much effort. Now I get very tired. Can I borrow your mascara? Your suit-case is empty! You're taking an empty case! A telephone book in it! What's become of you, you never went anywhere without your makeup."

"Please, mother, stop your crying, I can't stand it."

"Sorry, darling, I don't know why everything makes me cry. It's so sad. I have no one now. All the rooms are empty. Perhaps I'll take in a paying guest. Some one who will be glad to have a home, a hot meal at the end of the day. I'm a good cook, everyone says so. No. I don't want to be tied. Unless it's some one who will appreciate a clean bed. No girls. Girls are always washing their hair, washing their underwear, washing,

washing. If he won't expect too much, because you know I tire easily. All those thoughts, they wear me out."

"Sit down, on the bed over there. Now listen. Use your head. You're a smart woman. I mean it, despite everything. Why don't you get an interest, an intellectual one, that will keep the squirrels from running around in your head? Algebra, for instance. All those lovely x's and y's and z's to preoccupy you."

"You're making fun of me. You sound just like your father. Algebra! No one understands how I feel. I expected that you... after all you've gone through...some sympathy...you're humoring me...algebra!"

"I'm serious. Just imagine the beautiful symmetry of those simultaneous equations, the inevitability of their logic: if this be so, then it must follow that such be such, the balance is perfect, the conclusion irresistible. You take all those unknown and make them known. What could be more satisfying. Daddy always said the mind must expand."

"Just you be careful you don't take after him. His mind expanded until it cracked."

"He's doing fine, better than the rest of us."

"A fugitive, living on tortillas. He should be ashamed of himself, a girl younger than his own daughters."

"You had your day in the sun."

"I knew it, I knew the day would come when you'd blame me."

"I'm not blaming anyone, it's too late for that, I'm just saying you had your good times."

"I'm old and there's nothing to look forward to. My only comfort is the jig-saw puzzles. The pictures are so lovely when all the pieces are in place."

"O.K. When I get back, I'll buy you some new puzzles."

In two years' time, when her husband is away in Mexico City with the Canadian mayor, Raquel will recall her terror at the wedding. She will slip into the gardener's cool dark shack at the end of the garden and talk to him about her fears, although she will not be able to name them. They will sit side by side on his narrow cot, agreed that the mayor's visit is an omen of evil. The visitor arrived on the Day of the Dead. He is the color of a corpse, he speaks without opening his mouth, his eyes look out and reflect nothing; but when he thinks he is not being observed, stares at Raquel, and her sister, and mother, even Lupita, the laundress, as if to enter their souls. What if he casts a spell on the padrone and takes him away, what will become of us? Alfredo will comfort Raquel on a blanket spread out on the earthen floor. That day, she will get pregnant. The baby, a girl, will look like Raquel, very dark, with delicate bones and large eyes. Eventually her husband will find it necessary to discharge Alfredo because the gardener disobeys repeated orders to stay away from the padrone's house, out of his living room, out of his kitchen, refusing to keep to his quarters when not gardening. But he will have to pay him a year's wages first, in accordance with laws protecting servants. Raquel will always remember Alfredo's words: "Your husband reads too much, he thinks too much. That is why he has lost the machismo."

Sleeps the captain exhaling sibilants with every breath. Beside him Judith is wide awake, thinking, despite my horoscope, he does not want to see me again.

Sleeps the father of the bride. Beside him Raquel urges a breast upon her sleeping infant, perhaps to comfort herself.

Sleeps the old lady, like a feverish child, unhappily, not knowing any longer the difference between waking and sleeping.

Downstairs, the mirrors are empty.

Upstairs, a dresser mirror reflects an empty champagne bottle and two glasses.

Tony is observing a rite of his own. With Edie in his grandmother's massive nuptial bed. She, at one point, dozes off.

— What did you say? Yes, it was a strange evening. Yes, I am somewhat tired. The tension. It made me nervous. Nothing wrong. But things did not go as smoothly as usual. I was uneasy right from the beginning.

Under the covers, he is embracing her. Impassioned. At the same time trying to practice restraint: above all, avoid anxiety. That is what Edie has told him, again and again. He tries to feel nonchalant: tosses a few words into the conversation. Without giving up a single breath of his deep excitement, saying,

— There was no music. I can't understand anyone not wanting music at her wedding.

— No one listens to music any more, so why bother.

— I always listen.

— That's because you love music.

— I might have been a musician.

— You still can be a musician. Your mother's violin is upstairs.

— No. Not the violin. You have to get callouses on your finger tips. My mother did.

— The piano then. Or the flute, the sitar? What? I could arrange to have you take lessons. You should have an interest, then you wouldn't get so depressed.

She keeps wanting to help me...

Turns away, on his back, hands behind his head.

— You agreed: no discussions. I've been analyzed and talked at out of existence. You know what I want. Every night. You promised when you moved in here. I can't do it if you're going to keep reminding me. There...feel...lost it...

— Sh, not to worry. Turn out the light. Come to mama. Mama will kiss it better.

Edie slides down. Strong steady sucking.

— Please...let me...just this once...

— No! That's what the bathroom's for.

Tony running to the (adjoining) bathroom, where he masturbates. Ejaculates into a (blue) towel hung on a separate rod.

An hour later Tony switches on the light.

— There's someone at the front door.

She nods as if she had not yet slept. It is understood that Edie looks after all callers, night or day.

On the other side of the door voices rise and fall in an argument of some sort.

Sits bolt upright in bed. Is it the bride? Judith seeks comfort.

And in the dark, even as he vigorously and passionately makes love to the girl beneath him, it is the delicate sad face of his wife which is imprinted on his retina. He sees her in the doorway of his house in Cardiff holding out her arms to him. Continues his pumping steadily and rhythmically, aware that his partner is making small noises of pleasure, yet he is thinking...

...and we will rush at one another, hug and kiss like lovers, she holding on to my hand, showing me the new things around the house, telling me stories about the children, the neighbours, her father, my father. We will chat this way until we go to bed. In bed she is affectionate. Then, sometime in the night, she becomes, in my mind's eye, one of the others. I go ahead like a machine. She knows: she is resigned. Afterwards, we do not speak. We sleep. In the morning we have breakfast like old buddies. When the time comes for me to sail she wishes me luck and a safe return. I am happy to leave...

— A penny for your thoughts, Judith says.

The captain is very tired. He thinks, here it comes...

— Will I see you again, she persists.

— Shall I lie?

— No.

— I do not intend to see you again.

Out in the street the orphan couple is forced to run two blocks to where their car is parked: no one had left a space for them near the house. They run, they duck, they laugh, as if a crowd lined the sidewalk throwing rice and old shoes. But there is no one. The street is empty. Halfway down the block a backward glance reveals nothing, not even a hand at a window. Just the same they keep running as if eager to be off and away into a fun-filled future. The groom darts ahead and opens the door for his breathless bride. Inside the car the air is cold and damp as in a cellar, yet they feel safe, prepared to withstand a siege if necessary. The car is sanctuary. There are two motor rugs, two sets of fleece-lined boots; potato chips in aluminum bags; two plastic trays clipped to the dashboard fitted with plastic cups and plates; a bottle of Courvoisier in the glove compartment. The groom puts on red woollen gloves, curves his hands around the wheel.

— Where shall we go? he asks.

— Nowhere. Just drive around for a while.

— We could check into a motel for a while.

— No. They all know me.

— But this time it's different—you're married.

— They won't believe it. They will still treat me like dirt.

— Whatever you say. How long are we supposed to stay out?

— Until everyone is gone. About one, I guess. Edie closes the bar at midnight.

— Oh dear, that's more than three hours. We'll have to

113

keep the motor running, for the heater. That's dangerous, we must keep each other awake.

— Don't worry, we'll manage. I know a good car game. Have you ever played "Who Killed Cock Robin"?

— Leon and I played it all the time. He's in Spain now.

Driving through streets as familiar as childhood friends: west to Duplex, north to Highfield, east to Bessborough, south to Portland, west again to Yonge, down Yonge all the way to the lake, the red and green traffic signals keeping him alert, something to put his mind to. But unable to shut out the echo of the name. Leon. Leon. Wherever you are, I did it for your sake, this sham, this charade, it's all for you . . .

The bride thinks it was a lovely wedding. Hers.

— You looked beautiful, he assures her.

— Did I really? I hope they will remember me in white. It was wonderful to take that slow walk down the aisle on Thomas' arm. I hope Luba takes good care of my dress. The lace wasn't easy to find, it's genuine Val lace.

— She will. You can count on her. She was looking for Spence when we left. I wonder what happened to him, he was supposed to take her home.

— He must have passed out somewhere.

— Spencer was very nervous in the chapel. During the ceremony he stumbled all over the place, all over his own feet, all over my feet, a couple of times he actually got in front of me. I didn't mind, but Dr. McCauley had to keep pushing him out of the way. Spence froze when he was supposed to hand me the ring. At one point, I wondered if he was trying to take my place. If he and I had changed places, would it have made any difference to you?

— Of course. I wouldn't marry any of them now even if they wanted me. Whatever happens, we have each other. Try and forget Leon. You'll find someone else.

His eyes blink in his small face, sending signals into the darkness beyond. Leon why did you abandon me . . .

Car windows covered with steam, except where the wind-shield wipers have cleared an arc, through which lights can be seen in the distance, on the other side of Grenadier Bay. Perhaps, at this hour, they are bathroom lights left on for children or hall lights for the elderly.

The bride. Half asleep against his shoulder. Her legs are jackknifed up on the seat. She has been wrapped up in the two blankets from neck to toe like an infant, both arms inside.

The radio plays sentimental tunes. Nostalgia descends gentle as summer rain, washes away sins, removes stains, bleaches pain. Love is possible. The disc jockey blesses all lovers listening at this hour. Then he ends the benediction with the exact time and weather report. Assurances are with-drawn. All bets are off. Until the next record starts and longing begins all over again.

Father. When you spoke to me to-day it was the sound of Indian summer. Where were you when I needed your voice to dance to. Father.

The groom. Sits upright, his cold feet braced against clutch and brake. Hot air from the heater makes him nauseous, gusts of icy air hit the back of his neck. Yet he must keep a window open for safety's sake.

Leon. While I shiver here, you lie in the sun rubbing the belly of a beach boy. Leon.

Simultaneously bride and groom turn and hold on to one another when the radio plays Five Hundred Miles From Home.

— Is it time?

— Almost two o'clock.

— I hope the coast's clear. They must not know we haven't left town.

The house is in darkness, except for the old lady's bedroom, whose light is kept on night and day. The barred window casts a hop-scotch pattern onto the driveway at the side. The old lady, who is beating her fists against the bars, can be seen only if one happens to look up from the driveway. The couple does not see her, for they are at the front door. He asks her for the key.

— I thought you had it, she replies.

— I thought you got the key when you paid Edie.

Surely we are expected, they tell one another, everything has been paid for. Dare they ring the bell?

— Edie showed me the room I rented. She calls it the Versailles Room. It's very elegant. All gold and white. There's a huge canopied four-poster. Silk sheets. Velvet towels. And mirrors all over.

— Did you notice if there's a desk? he asks.

— No desk. Only the bed and mirrors and gilded chairs and a thick white rug.

— I wish there was a desk. There's a meeting on Monday afternoon. I must have those drawings ready. Just to be prepared. Carole will try and scuttle me if she gets to the boss first.

A door opens.

Inside, everything has changed. The couple stands uncertain in the empty front hall. The bar has disappeared. The folding chairs, the cheap glass ashtrays, the thick tumblers, all have disappeared. The smell of smoke and perfume has been replaced by disinfectant. Imprints of bodies against cushions, footprints on rugs, are gone. The mirrors are empty. Silence.

Edie stands before them, stern, tying the cord of her flannel dressing gown. Without her wig, thin strands of graying hair stand out from her head. She reproaches them:

— You have no right to disturb me at this hour. I kept your room until check-in time. When you didn't show, I was forced to rent it to someone else.

— I paid you for that room, the Versailles Room, the one you showed me when I paid you.

— As I recall, you bought Nuptial Number Three. That covers a Wedding Reception Deluxe, with the option of an overnight in whatever room is available. Rarely does a Deluxe couple exercise their option.

— Then why did you show me the Versailles Room?

— Why not. It's a gorgeous suite. I'm proud of it. Who knows: you might want it for some future occasion.

Just in time the groom catches the swaying figure of his bride.

— Hurry, he urges, can't you see she's not feeling well. Who's in there, perhaps they've finished, I'll give him his money back.

— If I were to interfere with every couple using my rooms, how long do you suppose I'd stay in business. Once the rent is paid and the door locked, I respect the rights of those who pay. — She takes hold of the bride's arm and pulls-pushes her up the steps. On the second floor landing, she points to stairs leading to an attic. — There are two empty rooms up there. Take your choice.

There is no choice. The rooms, one on either side of a little hall, are identical. Each has a low ceiling, slanted walls and a small window, furnished with only a three-quarter bed, table, lamp and a wooden kitchen chair. The groom guides her into the room on the right because he is right-handed and always turns in that direction. The room is cold and airless. There

117

is no light overhead, and no bulb in the lamp. Only the light from the hall.

— It's understood then? she asks.

— Yes, yes of course we've agreed, he assures her.

— You won't regret...?

— No, not I, it's you who might...

— Never.

— If you change your mind, it will be alright...

— I told you I will never let a man touch me again...

— Please don't upset yourself you promised...

— Darling I trust you...

— And we will have children...

— In about a year. I'll go away, disappear, lock myself up somewhere and come back with the baby. That will help you, won't it? It will throw them off—they will think you have become a father. No one need know the truth.

— I'll have to tell Leon.

— If you must. And I'll have my babies back, poor wee bastards, pushing their way out of bloody wombs, filling their lungs, not knowing their fate.

— We'll make it up to them for having been born.

The rest of the night is spent lying fully dressed on top of the cotton bedspread, covered only with their greatcoats. They sleep fitfully. He keeps waking up, reaching for her hand and holding on to it as if to restrain her from leaving. In the middle of the night, his delicate snores wake her. Her heart pounds for a long time as she stares into the dark, turning her head now and again, as if to establish her whereabouts.

Daylight is still feeble at the window when husband and wife stir in wakefulness. They appear to sense one another's intention, for they simultaneously leave the bed, put on their greatcoats and go out from the room. In the shadows of the little hall (someone has turned out the electric light) they whisper:

— Ready?

— Ready.

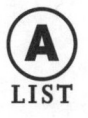

LIST

The A List